THE STONES OF
GREEN KNOWE

THE GREEN KNOWE CHRONICLES

THE STONES OF
GREEN KNOWE

L. M. BOSTON

Illustrated by Peter Boston

AN ODYSSEY/HARCOURT YOUNG CLASSIC

HARCOURT, INC.

Orlando   Austin   New York   San Diego   Toronto   London

www.HarcourtBooks.com

First Harcourt Young Classics edition 2005
First Odyssey Classics edition 2005
First published 1976

Library of Congress Cataloging-in-Publication Data
Boston, L. M. (Lucy Maria), 1892–1990.
The stones of Green Knowe/Lucy M. Boston.
p.   cm.
Summary: While eagerly following each stage of the new stone manor house
his father is building to replace their old wooden Saxon hall, a young boy,
part Saxon and part Norman, becomes involved with ancient magic
that carries him through time.
[1. Time travel—Fiction.   2. Magic—Fiction.]   I. Title.
PZ7.B6497Sr   2005
[Fic]—dc22   2004060588
ISBN-13: 978-0-15-205560-8   ISBN-10: 0-15-205560-6
ISBN-13: 978-0-15-205566-0 (pb)   ISBN-10: 0-15-205566-5 (pb)

Printed in the United States of America

A   C   E   G   H   F   D   B
A   C   E   G   H   F   D   B (pb)

THE STONES OF
GREEN KNOWE

One

For almost a year already Roger had watched the thick stone walls of the new house going up. All the time he was impatient and excited because he knew that it was going to be a marvel, it had been talked of for so long. So far, except for its tremendous solidity, it was not so very different from their old Saxon hall. It had arrow slits for windows and two rows of wooden pillars down the middle which would support the upper floor. It had no door. If he climbed up the builders' ladder outside and down inside, it felt like being in a prison, or perhaps in a very safe place. It depended on what game Roger was playing. He had never seen a stone house, and this one was to have two floors, an upstairs and a down. What could be grander? They would live on the upper floor, and the entrance door would be up there, up a flight of outside stairs. The ground floor would be for storage only. It was hard to imagine. All the houses in the village were either timber or wattle-and-daub. The hall his family had lived in till now was log-built, solid and dark and smoky. Its walls and rafters were painted in bright colors, but the smoke from the fire in the center of the floor blackened them as it curled its way up to the hole in the roof which served as a chimney. If, on a bitterly cold day sitting on the river bank with his fishing line, Roger thought of the great comfort of being back again in the house, the smell of wood smoke, and food, and people, and wet dogs, and straw and stable (for the four white oxen and the best horses had their stalls in with the family), came to mind as the coziest thing imaginable.

The Saxon hall was the center of the manor estate which Roger's father, Osmund d'Aulneaux, held under the Norman earl, whose daughter, the lady Eleanor, he had married. Originally the hall stood on a piece of ground half enclosed by a small backwater of the river. In the troubled time when King William Rufus died, Osmund had had the watercourse deepened and widened into a moat, cut off from the river and palisaded on the inner side. In case of attack the villagers and all the cattle could take refuge inside.

"No sensible man," Osmund said, "expects peace to last. But I hope this new house will. The church was built by the earl as a thanksgiving for the return of his son from the Crusade. What will our Bernard think when he comes back safe and sound from the fighting and finds his mother living in a fine stone manor house ready to welcome him?"

He said this to comfort his wife. Bernard, their eldest son, had gone as a page to the earl's brother who still lived in Normandy. There had been much fighting there, and no news had come from him for six months. His mother thought of him day and night. He had been sent away to the earl's household when he was only eight. It was the usual practice for the eldest son to be brought up by more important relations both to give him a better position and to bind the families together, but the lady Eleanor had never got over the parting. No other son could make up to her for her first-born. She was stern with her two daughters, and they took it out of Roger whenever they had the chance. The pages of the house were older than he. They spent their free time joking with the girls, playing such games as Blind Man's Buff that gave a chance of cuddling, or just making silly jokes, so Roger was rather left out. His grandmother was the one who loved him most. She was Osmund's mother, a Saxon of high birth. She lived in what was now her son's house, but it had been hers all her married life. Her Norman daughter-in-law, the lady Eleanor, looked down on her as a mere Saxon. This was always noticeable, because though the old lady had learned to speak

French from her girlhood when she was given in marriage to a Norman, she never spoke it like a Norman-born. She loved her son, and after him all her affection was for Roger. She told him the old Saxon legends and stories, in which often the Normans were the enemies and did not always get the best of it, and she told them in her native English which best suited their racy style. This had to be confidential between her and Roger, as the lady Eleanor did not approve. In Norman families French was the proper language. English was for the natives, the lower orders. But the grandmother too was proud of her birth, and she loved her native land as a conqueror never could. She taught Roger that he had famous Saxon ancestors and that love of this particular place ran in his blood. Roger was the second son, eleven years old, just at the age to be most interested in the builders and their work. There is no stone in the fenlands, so it had to be brought from a quarry in the midlands. There it was loaded into barges and came down the river easily enough following the current. On arrival near the manor it was loaded into carts and drawn by oxen to the site. Usually Roger spotted the barge as it appeared round the bend in the river far upstream, and he saw the unloading through with as much keenness as if he were in charge.

The walls were built of rough stone, carefully bedded and fitted together, but the larger blocks were tooled on the spot to fit corners and window ledges and arches. The master mason was very tolerant with the lord's son, and perhaps he would have been with any boy. Roger was allowed to try his hand. He was shown how every stone has a grain like wood and must be placed with the grain lying horizontally, or it will split. The mason handled the stone lovingly.

"There's good stone and bad stone," he said, "you could say it's living. Put your hand on a natural boulder warm in the sun, you can feel it's not dead, like bone for instance. The sun makes no difference to bone. Some pieces of stone are by nature bad, you can't do anything with them, and some are solid and loyal and will last for ever. Besides that, stone takes something from what it is used for. I've got a piece here that's going into your wall. It didn't come from the quarry but from a stone merchant. It came out of a little church that the Vikings burnt down. It has got a Saxon cross on it. I'm keeping it for the upper room."

Usually Roger spent the morning learning the arts of knighthood, for he would be a fighting knight when he grew up. He was dressed in imitation armor of stiff leather, and carried a wooden shield, and then on horseback practiced the rudiments of the kind of fighting peculiar to knights. He would have to be a skilled and daring rider, and also to understand hawking. His sisters also rode and hawked, but demurely on led horses, for they sat sideways. Now in the commotion of building, they, poor girls, were kept indoors spinning and weaving and embroidering with fine bone needles all the linen that would be needed for the grander house. They envied even the milk-maid who went out into the meadow at milking time, for cows were not brought into the byre, but, Norman fashion, the girl went out with a yoke across her shoulders and two wooden buckets and sought out each of the cows scattered across the common to milk it where it stood.

Unlike his sisters, Roger was at a loose end. When he had had his riding lesson and groomed his pony he must find occupation for himself. The building had been going on for such a time that he was beginning to lose interest, but when at long last the builders reached the upper level his enthusiasm was strongly revived. He was thrilled with the pulleys for lifting the large stones of the window-heads into place. He longed to be allowed to be one of the team who hauled on the rope to raise them, to have a hand himself in making these windows, which seemed to him, who had hitherto known only small slots between wooden uprights, the most glorious light-giving

invention. He had seen them of course in the new church, but to have them in the house where he was to live was almost unthinkable. When he saw the first one in position in the still-roofless wall, its arch and the two lights silhouetted against the sky, and a huge white cumulus cloud towering behind it, his heart leapt with pride.

He could not always stay to watch these wonders, although he was not troubled with any school learning. His younger brother Edgar was at the Abbey learning to read and write in Latin, and one in the family with this useful knowledge was considered enough. If Roger could ride, hawk, shoot, count, say his prayers, play his flageolet and mind his manners, that was all that was required from the lord of the manor's second son, and of these perhaps manners were the most important.

However, although the lord and his family did no manual work, his father expected Roger, as a youngster, to make himself useful in an emergency, and one of his occupations at the moment was watching over the flocks, because the shepherd's son who would normally do it was old enough to carry buckets and push barrows to help the builders. The lady Eleanor disapproved, saying herding was work for serfs, not for an earl's grandson, but Osmund held that there was nothing degrading about it. It was a clean job and it would get the boy away from bothering the builders. "He'll learn more bad language from them than he will from the sheep."

"That's true," said his mother. "He talks nothing but English now."

Roger set off with his dog Watchet early in the morning, let the sheep out of the sheepfold, and passed the long hours as well as he could with piping, carving little boats with his knife, climbing trees, gathering herbs for his mother, or practicing handsprings which he had seen acrobats doing at the Midsummer Fair. Nevertheless, a careful watch had to be kept, for there were buzzards that could carry away young lambs and in the nearby woods and the more distant forest there were foxes, polecats, and wolves. Watchet could be relied upon to deal with the first two. Wolves seldom came except in hard winters, but if one did, Watchet would tackle it and Roger would have to go for it with his knife or staff. He had never yet had to do this, but the thought of it gave him a sense of responsibility. He had followed a wolf hunt several times on his horse. He knew that wolves were only a wild kind of dog, and when it came to fighting Watchet was as savage as any.

The day seemed endless. Roger could hear in the distance the sounds from the builders, the masons' rhythmically tapping hammers, commands shouted down from the walls or his father's voice calling up from below, then a babel of voices as they all stopped work for the midday meal. Roger ate his bread and goat's cheese and felt left out. Even the singing of a sky full of larks, emphasizing all the emptiness, made him feel lonelier.

However, the afternoon was enlivened by a fight between Watchet and a stray dog. This was spring-time and dogs were roaming. At the sight of this guilty and furtive truant Watchet's neck and back rose in bristles and he went instantly into action. The sheep scattered, and then gathered into a group to watch with surprise a battle between their masters. It lasted some time, first furiously noisy, and then in deadly silence as each dog had its mouth full of the other. It is said that the dog on its own ground always wins. In the end the intruder limped off and Watchet, bloodied from tattered ears and a ripped shoulder, returned with a panting happy grin and bright eyes to Roger, having enjoyed himself greatly.

In the late afternoon the shepherd came to look over the flock and see that all was well. His dog Beth and Watchet were mates. Beth examined the signs of battle and Watchet boasted. The shepherd would spend the night there near the fold, keeping watch beside his bonfire. Roger was free to go home.

As he neared the house he saw that another window had been finished, two splendid windows now in the west wall, the stone colored rose by the setting sun.

The builders had a settlement of huts in the nearest field where at night they sat around the fire and told stories about their travels, for stone builders were few and journeyed far along the waterways. Men from the village joined them to hear their news and gossip, and Roger, when he could slip away from the family, loved to sit and listen. The talk was of robbers, of feuds and ambushes, of knavish men in high places. Also of the fearful accidents following on carelessness; how you must never walk under a ladder; and that if you have provoked the Fates by boasting, you must immediately touch wood because that is what the Holy Rood was made of. They told of the strange prophetic behavior of animals and birds, and the awful doings of demons. With so eager a listener as Roger their tales grew more dreadful and wonderful. Some miracles also they told, as of a church wrecked by members of the old heathen religion but rebuilt in the night by angels, accompanied by celestial music which, traveling along the water as music does, was heard far away over the fens.

There was a long period of warm spring weather, during which the building went on without a pause.

When Roger set off at five in the morning the bird-song was deafening, as loud as would be later on the noise of sheep and their lambs calling for one another all day in the meadow. The river was alive with many kinds of duck chasing each other round with splashing and frantic quacking. They took off in dense flights as he approached. Herons were fishing, swans circling with whistling wings, coming down with their webbed feet held before them like buffers to break the speed of their swish into the water. Along the river bank rabbits thudded and scampered at the sight of Roger and Watchet, hares went leaping away far too fast for a heavy dog to follow. In all the banks and brakes, birds and animals rustled about their business. From the earth upward there was a continuous everchanging pattern of life, of budding and unfolding, of nesting and feeding, of meticulous grooming, of calling to mates or young, of hiding, watching, and hunting. Roger was a watcher, too, as patient as any. There was a pool upstream where he could watch the young otters playing. He had seen the badgers carry out their soiled winter bedding and take in fresh bracken for the new season. He knew where the adders sunned themselves by the river, and where the flashing kingfishers had their holes. Sometimes he surprised deer at the edge of the forest before they bounded into cover. The forest had its own sinister population. More dangerous than wolves and bears was the wild boar that hid in the marshes.

Early in the morning when Roger relieved the shepherd from his night-watch and was alone under a sky streaked primrose and lilac by the sunrise, he felt that he, a human, was the rare occasional creature, while the whole world teemed with millions of other species living out their different lives, apparently with enjoyment but never without most watchful care.

At midday he lay in the May sunshine. The warm ground under him was his own, the winding stretch of river with the forest nearly coming down to it, his own, the honeybees and the flowers they swung in, his, and soon the tall new house, spacious and light, would be his for all his life. His brother Bernard would inherit from the lady Eleanor lands in Normandy, Edgar would have a small estate not far away, but Roger's portion of the inheritance was to be this land on which he had been brought up.

He had brought a sack with him today because the cowslips were now in bloom. There were so many that he picked most of the day and filled the sack with the sweet lemon-scented flowers for his mother to make cowslip wine. He liked it better than mead, which the men drank.

Going home at sunset was always an exciting anticipation. What would have been done on the house during the day? The flight of steps up to the future doorway had been made as the walls rose. Now he could run up, and walking like a cat along the beams and joists of the floor, which would not be boarded till the roof was on, could try to get the feel of the hall, and look out of the windows as if he already lived here. Beside the latest window he noticed the stone with the Saxon cross on it which the master mason had shown him. When he turned his back to the window and looked at the inside, it was shadowy and uncertain in the dusk, and as Roger held his breath it seemed to him that, less than half finished as the house was, the future was already there.

The base of the hearth had been built, not in the middle of the room with no vent for smoke except the hole in the roof as was usual, but in the center of the main long wall. This was a revolutionary idea. Round the campfire at night the older men strongly disapproved. How could you sit round a fire if there was only one side to it?

The master builder said, "How could you put a fire on a wooden floor? You forget it is upstairs."

"What do they want an upstairs for, instead of staying among their own people as is right and comforting for both?" asked one of the house servants who had joined the group.

"Perhaps to get away from your snoring!"

"Go on! Or the oxen blowing. And that's a good sound to hear in the night."

"Look how much clear floor space you get," said the master builder. "The hall will seem twice as big with the fire at the side."

"Yes, but only the people on one side of the table will be warm."

"Ask the steward to put you on the warm side, old bones. And there won't be any smoke to make you cough worse in the winter. This is the newest thing. We built one for the Bishop."

Roger was proud that his father was so ambitious and adventurous.

The hearthstone was to be laid next morning and he was to be present for the ceremony. The hearth from all time was the center and heart of the family. Under it would be placed a piece of silver, a piece of iron, and in a cavity a live toad. The silver was for wealth, the toad (because it was believed to live for hundreds of years) for permanence, and the iron to keep away the Little People, a smaller race of men who lived here before the Romans drove them out. They had lived in green knowes, which were dugouts roofed with a dome of turf, looking inconspicuous like a natural mound. Though they were small people they were good friends to have and bad enemies, for they could do magic. You never knew where they were.

There might even be some in the forest still. Wood-cutters told strange tales. Fortunately the Little People were afraid of iron. The old English name for the village was Green Knowe, but the Normans called it Turbeville, village of turf. In the end, as Roger was to find out, the old name was the one that survived.

The family gathered together to watch the laying of the hearth, the lady Eleanor with the grandmother and the girls at the top of the steps, the boys on ladders and beams. Some planks were put across for Osmund, the master builder, and the master mason to stand on, and the big hearthstone was hauled up by manpower on the pulleys and lowered into place. When it was straight and set, and the master builder had raised his hand in sign of approval, Roger crossed the beam to where his father stood and dropped on his knee in sign of obedience and loyalty. Osmund kissed him and afterward his wife and daughters, and everyone went away for a special breakfast with a double ration of mead for the workmen and serfs. Then work began again.

Two

The shepherd's boy now was sent back to the flock, and Roger was bidden to take four horses to the smithy to have them shod. The smith was descended from the Norsemen. His name was Olaf Olafson and he was a freed-man who lived in the village. He was a skillful craftsman who made not only horseshoes, bits, stirrups, and axes, but he could repair armor and make swords and scythes and intricate and beautiful hinges for doors, and in fact anything that could be made of iron.

Roger, watching him dangle from his tongs a strip of red-hot metal, of which he was making a ring in the shape of a coiled snake for a sword belt, asked him who had first thought of such an unlikely way of treating rock, for he knew iron came out of rock.

"One of the old gods it was who first showed men how to do it. They could never have found out for themselves. That's why there's magic in it." Olaf deftly manipulated the almost liquid metal thread. "You'll have heard of Weland's magical sword, so thin and pliable he could circle it round his body. And of Excalibur, King Arthur's sword."

"And then," said Roger, who had heard it from a traveling scholar monk, "there was the Emperor Constantine who had his stirrups and bridle-bit made out of the three nails of the True Cross."

"Ay, maybe, but that was Christian magic. There's older than that. Much older."

"Can you do it?"

"Some, my father taught me. But it's dangerous stuff. The priests don't like it. Nowadays smiths have forgotten it. They treat iron as if it was ordinary. So do I, mostly. But I know what I'm handling."

"Couldn't you do some little magic for me?"

"Such as?"

"Such as an arrowhead that couldn't miss its mark."

"Is that all? Just a little thing like that? Wouldn't I be popular. No, young sir. But leave me your knife and I'll put luck on it for you. There's no harm in that. Tie the horses up, and when you come back it will be ready for you."

"Can't I stay and watch?"

Olaf plunged the glowing ring into water. When it

had finished sizzling, his blue Viking eyes looked for the first time straight at Roger.

"What's secret is done in secret," he said.

It was no surprise to Roger that magic dwelt in so many things—stone and wood, and iron and wells, and hawthorn trees, and rings and cups, and even sometimes in woven cloth. Old tales were full of all these things, and old tales handed on by word of mouth from age to age were believed in as the gathered knowledge of the human race. There was no limit to what might happen. Although Roger's world was small and he had never yet been farther than a day's ride from home, if you lived on the outskirts of a great forest through which there were tracks here and there but no through road, and if all the tales you heard were of invaders and raiders and giants and werewolves and magicians, and if you lived on a river big enough for merchant ships to row up from the sea going to inland market towns, bringing with them strange men, strange tales, and rumors of wars, there would be no lack of excitement.

All these free reaches of the imagination were centered for Roger in the new house that would stand to repel invaders, to receive heroes, to outlast perils, to withstand in its living stone walls the evils of witches and demons. And now he who would live in it would fittingly own a knife with magic on it.

When Roger went back to fetch the horses, Olaf handed him the knife. It had been through fire, was a slightly more subtle shape and much sharper. On the broadest part of the blade was engraved a pattern of interlacing signs that looked like winged ash-tree seeds.

"There's your luck," he said. "Keep your mouth shut or you'll lose it."

Roger offered him a silver coin, but he refused it. "Magic that's crossed with money goes bad."

Roger rode home leading three horses, having in the sheath that hung from his belt a secret that filled his mind with hopes and questions. The first thing he did was to go into the ground floor of the new house and carve his initial on one of the wooden pillars that supported the beams for the upper floor. Underneath he copied as well as he could the pattern Olaf had put on his knife.

During the day the fireplace surrounding the hearthstone had been finished with decorated pillars at each side supporting an arch. The back of the chimney was corbeled out to give greater depth for the fire. All the villagers were coming in and out to marvel at this, to boast of what their manor house had, though they themselves lived in thatched huts with no light except through the doorway and the hole

in the roof. Even the church, though it had windows, had no fireplace.

Roger went out after supper to join the builders round their fire, for he respected their craftsmanship and found them amusing company. The mason was in the middle of one of his stories. He was the chief storyteller.

"For as you well know, I was born in France. My father came over to England with the de Greys. He was a mason, too. I was only a child at the time these things happened, but I heard the grown-ups talking. Well, as I was saying, this baron was as wicked a man as ever lived. He would swear a man's life away or starve a poor woman to death and never think about it again. He would commit any treachery for money, or even for no reason but the pleasure of it. They say he killed his son to spite his wife. A real devil of a man he was. In the end he had not an ally left, nor could he buy one for all his money. His enemies grew powerful enough to hound him out. He fled for sanctuary into this grand new church I was telling you of. My father was one of the masons working there. Now, among them there had been a certain sculptor famous for his craft. He had carved over the chancel arch the scene of the Last Judgement, the righteous rising up to heaven on one side and on the other the lost souls being thrust down into hell. In the center was God the

Judge with lightning in his hand. Now this sculptor could make stone come alive, so that people could not look at his carving without a feeling of holy fear. But the wicked baron that was sheltering there cared nothing for such things. As long as he stayed in sanctuary he was safe from his enemies, and he thought that surely money or blackmail or trickery would get him free. So he made himself as comfortable as he could for a night in the church. The place he chose for sleeping was the bottom step leading up to the chancel, because it was raised above the draught that blew along the floor from under the outside door. Little he thought of the Last Judgement just above him, but he cursed and swore at his enemies as he folded his cloak for a pillow and laid himself down, and he cursed again at the screech owls that sounded like demons besieging the church outside, and he cursed God Almighty for full measure.

"The sacristan came in in the early morning to prepare for Mass and there he found the baron lying dead, his body twisted and blistered and scorched black as if by lightning. It was difficult to find anyone brave enough to carry out the corpse that looked like the black Devil himself. However, because, though damned, the baron had been of the royal family, the Bishop decided, so as not to give offence, that he should be buried in the churchyard. A stone coffin was ordered for him. It was my father who made it. It took six men to move it on rollers to the shallow grave, and pulleys and levers to put it in. Then the corpse was laid in it, and six strong men heaved the monstrously heavy lid on top. Everyone was relieved when this evil creature was so securely boxed up and buried.

"Well, a month later it was All Souls' Day, and at Vespers the church was lit with a thousand votive candles and packed with people praying for the souls of their dead. There was solemn singing in the choir but outside the owls sounded like devils hooting and cheering, and things bumped against the glass of the windows. The congregation began to look round and forgot their prayers, and then they heard a human laugh as shrill as a horse's neigh, like the laughter of terror. And what was worst about it was that it had in it something of gratification. Also, to some of the congregation it was recognizable. It was in vain afterward that the priest gave the Benediction and said, 'Go in peace.' Nobody cared to go out. The choir however followed the clergy out into the vestry and thence into the churchyard, the men clutching each other in terror. There they found the soil thrown back and the stone lid of the coffin open. The body had gone. Not a pleasant thought that that was roaming about."

His hearers let out their held breath and shivered.

Then one added, "It's to be hoped that coffin was never used again, valuable as they are. Think of that lid now. It would be a fine piece of stone, very useful. A good threshold stone."

"No, no," said two or three voices. "Don't say such a thing. Stone remembers."

An old man, who had been asleep, picked up at the last words.

"I remember the Stones," he squawked. "They used to stand not far from here, on a bank beside the way to the Abbey. My grandfather lived here and he used to tell of them. Are they still there?"

"What manner of stones would they be?"

"Why, the Stones. Surely you've heard tell of them? Very old, they were. Sort of tooled, but not with iron; and strange they were. Two of them standing out alone on a grassy hill at twilight, it gave you the jumps to see them. Always called the Stones they was, but nobody knew what they were or how they came there."

"I know the way to the Abbey well enough," said another, "but the forest has encroached a fair distance on this side since it became the King's hunting. Maybe they are just lost in the undergrowth. No one round here seems to remember them. But then everything has changed since the Normans took over. Even the lord is not from here. Who would remember?"

Three

The roofing and the floor, and all the timberwork seemed to take as long or longer than the stonework, and was interrupted in the winter when there was a heavy fall of snow. When Roger got out of his bed one morning and looked out of the door of the old hall at a white world, the half-finished building under snow and seen through falling snow looked like the ghost of a dream. The snow continued for a week, and the builders left their flimsy huts to take shelter in the Saxon hall where there was little enough room already.

The high table at the end of the hall was a step up from the mud floor of the main part, on a paved dais that could be kept clean. The table always had a clean linen cloth, and though the family ate with their fingers, table manners were very particular. Serving, eating, and drinking at the high table were done with great style, not unlike the coming and going and genuflection of servers in the Mass. Behind the high table

were two curtained four-poster beds, one for the grand-mother and the girls, the other for the lord and lady and any important guest. Where everyone was so crowded together, it was the bearing and manners of the lord's family that distinguished them from the crowd with whom they mixed so closely.

"I shall be glad," said Osmund, sitting with his harassed and complaining wife just above the jostling and steaming mob, "when we have the new hall and this overcrowding can never happen again. We are herded like sheep."

It was late spring before the walls were plastered inside and out and the roof finished. A branch of yew was fixed to the roof-ridge to mark "the topping" and a great feast was held. All the builders, the manor servants, and the villagers ate in the old hall. The lord and his family, including Roger's uncle, the earl's son who had come for the occasion with his retainers, were feasting for the first time in the new hall in won-derful space and comparative privacy. The sun poured in through the windows and brought in with it the smell of sweet briar. Musicians played while the dishes were carried by pages in new clothes. It was a new way of living, it took Roger's breath away, but at the same time he had a sneaking regret for the boisterous enjoyment, the cracking of rude jokes and gales of laughter, that were going on in the old, dark fusty place where he had grown up. You could never have your horse with you here upstairs, nor wake up at night to see the shadows of the wide horns of the oxen thrown on the wall by the firelight. All the same, the grand new house was a proud place. His only real regret was that as it was spring they did not have a blaze in the new fireplace.

However, in the evening even this wish was fulfilled, and the fire was kindled to help to dry out the plaster. The hall was lit with dancing flames, and for the first time Roger heard the sound of fire fluttering, pulling, and leaping up a chimney, quite a different sound from a fire in the center with no directed draught.

"Do we sleep in here tonight?" asked the earl's son.

"Certainly we do," said Osmund. "The beds are new and good. I think you should sleep well." But he blushed a little, suddenly realizing that till now he had slept with the animals. The earl would think that quite barbarous, and indeed so now did he.

The end of the hall was curtained off for the bedchamber. The hangings were what the girls had been kept so busy all this time embroidering. These made a handsome background to the high table. In the body of the hall were tables and benches for the pages and the steward and other superior retainers, who would later make their beds on the floor. Roger as son of the house, though he slept with the pages, had his place at the upper end. He lay awake watching the shadows close down as the fire died. They waited in ambush under the timbered roof to rush out over the high walls, jumping back whenever a log collapsed and flared, lighting for a moment the beautiful arches; but they encroached more and more as he got sleepier. Watchet lying beside him, dreaming some dream of his own, beat the straw mattress with his tail.

It was an anticlimax when after so long all the builders had gone and their camp was empty. The usual spring occupations on the farm were going on as if nothing had happened, but the house was there, an unending wonder and source of pride to Roger. It could be seen, except in the forest, from all the country round. It was even more conspicuous than the church which stood a little farther downstream. When Roger went hunting or hawking with his father he sat his horse more confidently because he was the son of that house.

One morning Roger was out with Watchet. He liked roaming the country watching the birds and animals and noting where they lived, which can be done much better on foot than on horseback. Osmund, when they hawked together, respected his intimate knowledge, which was always helpful. This time Roger had crossed the river by ferry and was farther afield than usual following the edge of the forest. On the fringe, before the really big trees began, there was a round hill covered with a scrub of elder and hazel and brambles. Watchet had put up a rabbit that had bolted into cover there and Roger was watching a flock of young blue-tits while the dog dug and yelped and tore off roots to get lower into the burrow. When his excitement sounded distant and rather smothered, Roger began to think he might get so far in that he wouldn't be able to get out again. With his knife he started hacking away at the tangle of brambles under which Watchet had disappeared. He wished he had his hawking glove for he was soon licking the blood off his hands. He worked for a considerable time cutting a tunnel through which at last he saw Watchet's tail sticking out of a hole. He could have hauled him out by it, but instead let him go on enjoying himself down there, for his own attention had been caught by something else. He had twice hit his knuckles against stone. Boulders were unknown in these flat lands. Could it be some ruin? The builders had told him they were always on the lookout for mounds, under which heaps of good tooled stone could often be found. Roger's knife was so sharp it was tempting to cut away

one branch more, and then another, and then another, until he suddenly saw what he was uncovering. This was no corner of a wall, no builder's stone. It was a *stone chair,* all in one block, seat and back roughly chiselled. As Roger examined it, the old man's words came into his head: "tooled, but not with iron." The cutting-marks were not at all like the mason's, which were done with a toothed chisel, worked in slanting lines very evenly. Roger knew, he had watched and he had tried to do it. This seat was so primitive it looked as if the stone had been chipped off with stone.

In Roger's world people sat on wooden stools or benches. Only kings, bishops, and dukes sat on high-backed chairs, thrones really. There was not one in the manor house. But if this stone seat was for a king, it had no ornamentation however simple, as if the stone implement with which it was done could not make a beading or a symbol. Also, it was far too small. The back stood about four feet high, but the seat was low and child-sized. No fat bishop could ever have sat on that.

Roger went down on one knee before it as he would have done before a great lord, and passed his hands over the shape of it. It was as if his fingers could feel infinite oldness.

He stood up in great excitement. If there was a second one near by, he knew what he had found.

Watchet was backing out of his hole, tired and discouraged, so Roger pulled him free by his tail and himself went back to work. Sure enough, there was another stone quite near, exactly like the first but slightly smaller. He cleared that, too.

The Stones! Roger called them the King and Queen.

The sun was setting. As it dropped behind the forest the shadows of the trees leapt toward Roger as if to take him captive. He knew that the extent of the forest was vast and unmeasured, only nibbled at here and there where men had made clearings along the rivers of enough ground to support small farms and hamlets. Now suddenly the forest seemed darker, quieter and more expectant, even watching. This was no place to be in after dark. Roger had sometimes ridden home through part of it at twilight after visiting the Abbey with his father, amid a clatter of retainers, but now he was alone, more than an hour's walk from home.

The sun dropped out of sight, and instantly it was twilight. Roger turned to look at the two stones where they stood in the little clearing he had made, at the top of a mound. They received the twilight as if they had never been parted from it, never been hidden; as if they were as old as the setting sun. And yet, they had no business to be there, they made no sense. They filled him with misgiving.

The afterglow of twilight faded out, and with the dusk a nightingale began to sing, hesitant at first but soon in full song, to be heard for miles. Roger took heart. The nightingale's song was as old as the coming of summer after winter. He did not doubt it had started with the creation of the world. He did not need to fear things for being old. It was rather a reason for loving them that they had been there so comfortingly long, like hills.

Roger was glad that the brambles and brushwood he had cut and dragged away into a heap formed a blind, so that no one going along the track to the Abbey could see what was now standing on the slope. Evening was closing in, and he was likely to miss supper, at which it was his privilege and his duty to wait on his father. He would be scolded for this breach of manners and perhaps have to go to bed hungry, but he felt a deep satisfaction. He had restored to their rightful position things that had a hidden meaning. When the moon rose it would shine on them as it had done long before, and when the sun rose it would find them there.

Roger bowed to the Stones that stood in the half-dark like two people, then he set off for home. He was not afraid of losing his way where there were no roads but only green tracks. He knew it as his horse Viking did, and he had Watchet who also knew it. If across country in the dark he went wrong, he had only to slip a spare bowstring from his pouch through Watchet's collar and say "Home" and the dog would gladly tug him in the direction of the ferry. Watchet took great satisfaction in crossing the river by boat, and would bark to fetch the ferryman.

Four

That night Roger lay on his pallet and his thoughts kept him awake. The moon was shining in through the gable window. Its beam lit on his pillow and on the face of the page sleeping near him, but left the rest of the hall in darkness. Roger imagined the Stones standing together in its opal light like two living things, waiting. He slept and dreamt about them. He woke and his head was still full of them, but he did not mention them to anybody because he was afraid his excitement would be laughed at. Had his friends the builders still been there, he might have talked to them. Perhaps Olaf the smith could be trusted. When Roger was exercising his horse he rode down to the smithy. Olaf had just finished making a chopper and was fixing the blade into its shaft.

"Olaf, you remember that knife you did for me?"

"I do, master Roger."

"I want you to put a new edge on it. It's been doing a lot of work."

"Has it, now?"

"I oughtn't really to use it for cutting brushwood, but it is so sharp, it seems to tempt me."

"Ah."

"I'm afraid I've dented the blade. But it was very important."

"Maybe you found something."

"Yes. But I don't know what it's for."

"Ah."

Olaf took the knife and examined it.

"You've been rough, the two of you; you and the knife." He began work on it, holding it in the fire, beating the edge, putting it on the grindstone and finishing it with sand and oil.

"There," he said. "That will cut a feather in the air. But to finish your job you'd better take this chopper. It was ordered for the manor house anyway."

Roger thanked him and put the knife in its sheath and the chopper in the leather wallet that hung from his belt and rode off. Nothing had actually been said, and yet he felt reassured.

Norman nobles had a great reputation for rough riding. Roger always regretted that the flat country gave him little opportunity. Any slope that you could gallop up and down was good for the horse and for horse-manship. He was therefore excited by his discovery of the little hill, not steep enough to put a horse on its haunches coming down, but it had at least a stream to be jumped at the bottom and a line of loose brush-wood to be jumped at the top. If he rode there it would cause no comment since it was his business to exer-cise the horse, and he could be there and back quickly. He set off now with Watchet running happily beside him. He discovered that his little hill was ac-tually an island. The stream that ran through the for-est divided round it and then joined again to go on its way. When he came on foot, Roger had crossed it by a rickety plank for there was no bridge. This ac-counted for the fact that no sheep were pastured there and no plowing was done. No one in fact was inter-ested in this bit of land.

When he had explored round the edge of the island, Roger put Viking up the steepest side and jumped the line of brushwood, pulling up by the Stones. They looked smaller seen from horseback at midday, and less conspicuous. A peasant girl intent on cutting rushes, or a swineherd rounding up his provoking, self-willed pigs, more wild and agile than any sheep, might easily pass them as simply stones, without even wondering how they got there.

Roger had come to finish off what he had begun. He tied Viking to a tree and set to work with the chopper on the stumps and broken stems he had left. He made a neat clearing round the Stones so that they stood free, with a semicircle of small trees behind them and a good long brush screen on the side where the packhorse went toward the Abbey.

When he had finished, his imagination, as well as his back, was tired. It seemed to him quite ordinary to sit down on a stone.

Before him spread a wide view. He could follow the course of the river through all the land he knew, from upstream, through the common land and the cultivated strips, the orchards and spinneys and the osier beds, and so into the blue distance. Away down there he could see the manor house, its new white plaster catching the sun. Its gable was as tall as the church tower. It dominated the landscape even though at this distance it looked no bigger than an egg.

Roger let his mind wander over the expanse, fixing the places that he knew, the trees that he recognized. In that wood was a heronry, under that cluster of hawthorns a badger's set. His thoughts ran on by themselves. The stone that he was sitting on was the same kind of stone as the manor house walls. He supposed all stone was the same age, all dating back to

the day of the creation when God made the earth, so that really the windows of his house, though newly tooled, were as old as the Stones. They could last as long into the future as those went back into the past. He passionately wanted the new house to be there forever, as permanent where it stood as these stones on their hill. "I would like to see it," his thoughts ran, "a long time ahead, just to be sure, and to see who lives there then." His idle hands had plucked a dandelion head.

"I'll let this decide." He blew at the perfect sphere and a tuft of fluff flew off in a little cloud. "One hundred." He blew again and another tuft flew away. "Two hundred. Three hundred. Four hundred. Five hundred!" Only four threads were left. "I can't count those as hundreds. Say tens." He blew four times. "Five hundred and forty. I wish, just for half an hour, I could visit it in five hundred and forty years' time."

He could not have accounted for it, and it did not occur to him to try, but he found himself, with no memory of having walked there, approaching the manor house along the river bank. He was surprised that the fields seemed immeasurably wider, as if the forest had drawn back, and the herds of cattle were sleeker and fatter. And whose could be the immense flocks of sheep? Familiar landmarks like giant trees were missing. Even the course of the river had changed, and instead of the ferry there was a stout wooden bridge that would take two horses abreast. Roger wondered if he was dreaming, but he knew he could choose what he would do, which you never can in dreams, where everything relentlessly happens to you.

At a little distance he could see two people walking along who were dressed madly enough for any dream. Their clothes made them look like gaudy birds, with frills and loops of ribbon overlapping like feathers, especially round their necks, wrists, and knees. They had high-heeled shoes that made them strut like birds. They looked like pheasants with swords for tails. Their bulky clothes were also decorated with silver balls down the front, on the sleeves and pockets, and even in the small of the back. They had thick long hair in rows of regular curls. It would be impossible to wear a helmet over that yet they carried swords and so must be men. Roger knew that invasions of foreigners could happen almost without warning, but invaders would be wearing armor, not huge hats with feathers!

Roger hid himself to watch and to learn if he could what such strange creatures meant. As the two passed near him, strolling leisurely as if they owned the place, he could hear that they were not talking French, as he did, but English surely, except that these apparent grandees made it sound finicky and affected so that he could hardly prevent himself from laughing. They passed by his hiding place, near enough for him to watch with interest an unnaturally clean, beringed hand pushing the silver balls that decorated his clothes through slits in the cloth to keep them closed. What a good idea! Among Roger's acquaintances if you wanted your jerkin or your underclothes done up, you laced them, and for your cloak you used a brooch. When the two men had moved on, Roger continued toward the manor house.

From a distance it looked as he expected, except that the chimney stack seemed to be in the center of the roof. At first he thought it was just a trick of light and perspective that made it appear so, but as he got nearer he was obliged to believe that it really was so. "We can't have gone back to a fire in the middle of the floor again. That would be crazy. Though Grandmother did complain that it was cold at the high table."

He was walking toward a little wood that he knew very well, beside the river and not far from the house. At the edge of it a big horse was tied, which surprised him. Why did the owner not ride right up to the house? Roger entered the wood, and presently noticed a villainous-looking man in shabby earth-colored clothes lurking in the trees ahead of him, keenly watching something beyond. He had a rope in his hand as if to catch an animal. Roger became wary and drew near to see what he was after—one of his father's sheep or calves that had strayed, perhaps; in that case a thief. Roger crept nearer, but all that he could see was an enchanting little girl of about eight years old, frolicking about the wood picking primroses. Once she caught sight of Roger and smiled to herself—luckily not at him or the stealthy watcher might have looked round.

As she moved from one clump of flowers to another, she steadily got farther from the farm outbuildings and nearer to the hidden man, who gathered up his coil of rope and crouched low and ready. The child, shaking her curls and singing under her breath, knelt down by a big group of primroses with her back to him, and was silent as she picked, except for the tinkle of her bracelets.

Roger had never seen this girl before, but she was a darling and he would not see her hurt if he could help it. He drew his knife from its sheath. The man was too big for him to tackle any other way. As the wretch sprang out upon the unsuspecting child, Roger struck at the small of his back, but the knife skidded on one of the metal buttons, and instead of wounding him it neatly cut through his sword-belt and coat and ripped the string of his breeches, so that they fell round his ankles and bound his legs together almost as effectively as his own rope could have done. He stumbled and fell forwards and the brambles got tangled in his dishevelled clothes, also a branch swinging up whipped him in the eye. It would have been easy to knife him again, but as he struggled there ridiculously undressed, Roger felt more like laughing, though the man was angry and dangerous. Meanwhile the little girl had run away screaming for help. Roger felt strongly inclined to run away, too, and that gave him a good idea.

From the manor had come voices and calls, dogs barking, and general alarm. The villain, whatever he was after, had got to his feet. With one hand he clutched his breeches, the rope, his sword-belt and scabbard, with the other his bare sword, all very hampering for running in woodland, as he made off toward his horse. But Roger had thought of that and sped off a moment before him. He was younger and faster and uncluttered, so he reached the horse first, untied it, mounted it, big as it was, and galloped off leaving the man with no means of escape.

Roger rode round the edge of the wood giving the hunting "Hulloa," meaning to send his father's men and dogs out on the search. Someone however had already given orders. A tall boy in slim silken clothes was sending out men, presumably his own retainers, while the little girl was telling her story to two ladies, one young and one old, and a cluster of maid servants.

Roger rode up to them.

"I stole his horse," he said laughing. "He won't get far." He had spoken in French as all Normans did. There was a surprised silence, then the tall boy said,

"Do you not speak English?"

Roger reddened with anger, because he thought he was being treated like a servant; then he remembered the grandees he had passed on his way here. As he dismounted and made a courteous bow to the ladies, he repeated what he had said in English. The little girl laughed uncontrollably.

"What funny English!" she said.

"I see she has not been too frightened," Roger said to the mother. "I should hate anything to happen to her here. I suppose, ladies, you must have come with the earl? I did not know he was expected. If you are of his family then this little lady and myself must be cousins."

The little girl this time smiled fully at him.

"I saw you in the wood," she said. "I was glad you were there. Look, I shall put some primroses in your shoes, because you haven't any bows like we have."

She stuck a little bunch of primroses in the opening of each of his deerskin boots.

The tall boy looked Roger up and down, puzzled. To him the stranger's clothes were very odd, as primitive in shape as the poorest swineherd's but of good cloth, embroidered with crimson, and he wore a gold torque round his neck. His speech was uncouth, but his manners perfect.

"Who are you?" said the boy with the authority of one who is on his own ground.

"Toby, my dear," said the lady, "I think we should thank him. He saved my little Linnet."

Toby smiled at Roger and changed his manner.

"May I know who it is to whom we owe so much thanks?"

"My name is Roger d'Aulneaux, and I live here."

At his name they all looked at him in silent astonishment.

"Whereabouts do you live? I have never seen you before."

"Why, here in the manor, my father built it. Is he not at home? Or my mother?"

"I don't understand what you say," said the boy. "My name is Toby Oldknow and this is my father's house. And this is my mother."

She was beautiful and charming and held out her hand to Roger who dropped on one knee to kiss it.

"I am sure your mother is not here," she said. "What is her name?"

"My mother is the lady Eleanor de Grey, by birth. My father is Osmund d'Aulneaux."

"It is true, Toby my love; we have some connection with the de Greys, a distant cousinship."

Toby held out his hand. "Welcome then, cousin, the more for what you have done. But now I want to join the hunt for this man. I've sent for my horse. Where did you leave yours? I hope not anywhere where that scoundrel can get it? Or did you come in a carriage?"

A groom was leading up a chestnut horse that filled Roger with love and envy. It shone like a fox and danced about.

"Here's Feste," said Toby.

"Whew!" said Roger. "What a beauty! Has he Arab blood? Mine is a rough little horse but he can go. He's in the stables here. I didn't go out on him today."

As he said these words, the world began to spin round Roger. "No," he said, "that's wrong. I did go out on him. Then—"

Toby frowned. He disliked what he thought was stupid pretence.

Linnet pulled her brother by the sleeve. "Toby," she said, "don't be stupid! Can't you see he's one of *the others*? I knew at once."

But Toby galloped off, followed closely by the strange horse. It was only later that he noticed it was riderless.

Linnet ran to her grandmother and repeated, "Granny, he's one of *the others.*"

Her friendly little voice was lost in the insistent yelping of Watchet, jumping up to lick him as if after a long separation. Viking, tethered close at hand, whinnied and pawed the ground. Roger was sitting on the Stone feeling very peculiar. He was sure it hadn't been a dream. He sat with his head in his hands trying to remember exactly what he had done and seen. The smoke coming out of a central chimney. It wasn't possible that it could have been altered in a day.

And now he remembered, there had been big windows on the ground floor, and all the windows had flashed in the sun in a way he couldn't understand. Yes, it was like a dream. The old Saxon hall had gone and he hadn't even thought it odd. The chestnut had been brought out of a new stable with stone arches over the doors. Then those mad birdlike clothes on the two older men. Toby, being a boy, was more simply dressed, and his mother more beautifully than could be thought possible, though Roger's mother would think her very indecent, with no veil over her head and her dress cut so low that it showed her smooth shoulders and the upper part of her chest. Roger had been not so much shocked as dumbfounded at such loveliness. What had shocked him was having to talk to such a noble person in the language he used for

Watchet, serfs, and tradesmen, though of course also with his grandmother as an intimate secret, disguised as a joke.

He tried to remember how it began. He knew he had been sitting on the Stone, looking at the view spread out before him and thinking of the future of the house. An echo of his own voice now came into his mind saying, "I wish just for half an hour . . ." then his brain remembered the rest. He had wished to see if the house was there in five hundred and forty years time and who lived in it! He took his hands from his face, suddenly enlightened, and as he bent forward in excitement his hands, sliding down his shins to his ankles, met something nearly as soft as beaver. Primroses, droopy from a warm little hand! So it was real, not a dream. At least, they were real. But was he? Linnet had said in absolute confidence he was one of *the others.* Did she mean he was dead? Or who were they and how was he connected with them? Had they anything to do with the Stones? A shivery thought, for about the Stones he knew nothing except that they had powers. He felt a sudden panic lest by wishing the future he had banished the past and the house was no longer his to live in, though it was still there. He galloped off homeward, Viking being doubly willing after his long wait and with the usual desire to get

back to stable. Watchet caught up panting while they waited for the ferry.

How comforting to see again all the landmarks as he had left them this morning, and as he got nearer, to recognize the men working on the land. The house still had its stark walls with arrow-slit windows downstairs. The upper floor was still fresh from the builders' hands, sharp-cut with a sparkle in the grain of the stone from sheer newness. The windows had no magic reflection of the sun but opened into the soft half-darkness of the interior.

Joyfully Roger stabled Viking in the Saxon hall, fed him and rubbed him down. He greeted all the men about in the yard with a warmth that surprised them, and ran up the outside stairs three at a time to kiss his mother's and his grandmother's hands and grin at his sisters.

"You seem very pleased with yourself!"

"Not with myself, but I love this house. It's a good place to come back to."

"I'm glad you are back in time to wait at supper," said his mother. "Your father didn't say much the other night when you were late, but he was displeased. I didn't like to see a page taking your place. It was a disgrace to you."

After so strange an adventure, Roger felt he must talk to somebody, if only in a roundabout way. He hung around waiting for a moment when he could be alone with his grandmother. This was not easy in a house where everyone lived in one room. The girls were often whispering in corners, but the old lady was too dignified for that. However, this time he was lucky. His mother went down to the drawbridge to meet Osmund coming back from Huntingdon, and the girls ran into the courtyard to lark with the pages. His grandmother was sitting near the open door enjoying the evening.

"Granny, when you were a girl, did anyone tell you stories about the Stones? I mean the two that stand near the track to the Abbey."

"My dear boy! The Stones? Of course I remember them, but no one has mentioned them for years. Not since I was married. Who talked to you about them?"

"Old Karl the hurdle-maker was talking to the builders about them."

"There were many stories about them in the old days before the Conquest. My old nurse used to say that if you went at full moon you would see the Devil sitting on one and his witch-wife on the other, but my mother said it would be the King and Queen of the Little People and they would grant you wishes, show girls their future husband, and that sort of thing."

"Did you ever go and wish?"

"No, I never saw them, and when I heard of them

it was already nothing but a very old legend. The story was that people used to take them offerings of flowers, and pour libations. They were so much venerated by the people that the Abbot of that time who was very stern and unyielding decided it must stop, because of course they were heathen things, not Christian. So one All Hallows' Eve he set off with a boy server to exorcise the Stones. But he had hardly begun when a pack of wolves came for him out of the forest and he was eaten up, every bone of him. The boy escaped by swinging the censer against the wolves' noses. But after that nobody dared to go for fear of the wolves, and after a while the Stones were forgotten."

"Why did you never tell me about them?"

"Why, because if I had done you'd have gone straight to look for them."

"I've found them, Granny."

"You have? I might have guessed. Well, my dear boy, don't do anything to displease them. It is wise to be courteous to power when you meet it."

At this point all the family came in, and the conversation was ended. Osmund greeted his mother and they all prepared for supper.

That evening Roger waited on his father, offering on one knee the water and towel for hand-washing and afterward the meat, with a new style and confidence, simply because he had a secret.

"He does it already with quite an air," said Osmund to his wife. "I'm glad I wasn't too hard on him the other night."

Five

Roger's dreams were haunted by Toby's chestnut horse. Never had he seen anything so shining. Viking was a bay. He now got such curry-combing and brushing as never before, but his winter coat had never been sheared off so the new summer coat was rough. Neither had he Feste's fine dancing legs. Nevertheless, Viking was tough and much loved.

Day after day followed in which Roger had no chance to go off alone. First he had to accompany his father who was trying cases and hearing petitions in the manor liet court, held under a big oak tree. This was part of Roger's education. He had to learn what as a man he would have to administer. It would have interested him if it were not so very long-drawn-out. The peasants were as passionate as they were incoherent and repetitive. It was hard to get at the truth. The clerk had to write down the judgement, which he did very slowly, as if to make it clear to the ignorant that writing was magic and to be treated with reverence and given time to work. Once it was written down it had absolute power.

Roger liked to see his father held in such respect, and as he thought, giving very fair judgement; but his own sympathies were generally with the peasant who lost his case, or worse, was fined. The courts lasted several days, for when free speech is a right people tend to make the most of the occasion. It had the advantage that in the evenings over supper Osmund was often very funny about it, being a good mimic and tired of being so solemn and severe in public.

As a treat for Roger, who had behaved himself very creditably in court, Osmund took him and his sisters and the pages to Cambridge to watch some jousting on the grounds of the castle. Roger would have liked his father to put on his armor and take part, but he said in war he would charge against any knight, but was too old to do it for fun. However, they decked their horses out in their best bridles and colored cloths and themselves in their best tunics and jewels to make an appearance among the great crowd of nobles.

As all knights were of noble blood, of every two that competed one was likely to be of a family they knew, or knew to be among the earl's liege men, so they could always join in the shouting and applause.

The girls could scream when one whom they supported crashed to the ground in all his armor and lay there as helpless as a blackbeetle on its back until his squire ran to help him up. The bruises received by the defeated must have been remarkable, and a cause of much boasting and joking at home. The horses needed to be of a heavy build to carry the weight of metal and to withstand the shock of impact at full gallop. Roger thought his Viking would be better at it than Toby's deerfooted dancer if they should ever practice together.

All the time his father pointed out to him where the defeated knight had made a mistake, what the winner had done that he must copy, and made him learn to recognize the different coats of arms on the shields and banners. They met friends of the family and many young people. The girls were thrilled to speak to winners still in armor but without their helmets, looking so handsome.

They could not stay for the feasting and singing afterward because they had a long way home to ride before nightfall. They set off with quite a clattering cavalcade going the same way, but their companies separated, said "Good night," and turned off at different points on the road, till only their own party was left, too tired to talk. Dusk had fallen. It was difficult to see the road, which was only distinguished from open country by the deep ruts of wagons and dried trodden mud. A full pale moon was just over the horizon as they neared home and the weary horses broke again into a trot. The windows of the house showed rosy from the rushlights inside. Men ran out from the Saxon hall with candle lanterns to take the horses in.

The lady Eleanor stood at the door to welcome them, and chatter and commotion broke out again, the girls pouring out excitement to their mother and Roger to his grandmother, until the longed-for supper was served, and talk gave way to blissful eating. On the wall their father's armor and shield and lances glittered with little rushlight reflections and threw big shadows, that of the plumes of the helmet flickering as if they were blown in the wind. Roger's sleepy head was full of the sound of the heralds' trumpets, of neighing and galloping and the mad clash of collision between knights; and after the shouting had died down, in the momentary quiet, the clap of flags in the wind.

The next day the horses were given a rest, but after that the riding lessons were longer and more enthusiastic. Roger was allowed a heavier wooden shield and lance and a bulky leather jerkin, to try at the quintain—a hanging ring that he must take on the point of his lance as he galloped past. He was not riding Viking but a bigger horse trained for teaching youngsters. He was too young to have an expensive suit of armor that he would grow out of, or to tilt against a real opponent, even of his own age. It was hard enough to manage the shield and the reins in one hand and wield the long lance in the other. When he had galloped past the quintain ten times and speared the ring once, his right wrist was aching as if his hand might drop off. He was thankful when Osmund said, "That's enough for one day. You were not too bad."

Six

Roger had the pages and his sisters for company and could pass the time playing marbles, or backgammon, or chess, or walking on stilts, but his thoughts were always with Toby and Linnet and their beautiful mother. He could not speak of this strange experience to his family because no one would believe him. Perhaps he could have another word with Olaf. He went along to the smithy taking Viking who had loosened a shoe on the way back from Cambridge.

"Well, young sir," said Olaf as he bent over Viking's lifted foot, "I hope you've not been misusing that very sharp knife. I didn't give it you for stabbing people in the back."

Roger was startled and horrified. Was Olaf teasing him or did he know? When he put it like that, stabbing in the back was unknightly, and he *had* meant to do it.

"Your knife," he said at last, "has a way of its own. It got me out of trouble very neatly."

"So much the better." Olaf asked no questions but was busy fitting the new shoe.

"I've been going off, rather far, on my own."

"Ah."

"I was wondering if I could take Viking with me."

"I never heard of anywhere where a man could go and his horse couldn't, except scaling castle walls or climbing trees."

"Or," said Roger pretending the conversation was just fooling, "up a spiral staircase in a tower."

"You might get Viking up but I wouldn't like the job of leading him down."

"Oh, I would ride him down."

"Maybe you would. And sillier things than that. You'd jump him blindfold."

Something of that sort was just what Roger had it in mind to do, so he grinned at Olaf, and mounting Viking he cantered off toward the ferry, where he filled his leather bottle with water, then he followed the track toward the Abbey till he came to the Stones.

It was a still hot day. In the semicircle of trees and over all the forest there was a feeling of rising energy that could be kept down no longer! The gorse-buds were popping and the air was full of released fragrance and shimmering wildness. The birds, too, were trilling and whistling and cooing so loudly you might have thought it was to cover up what was going on. The Stones seemed to be waiting. Beside one of them a hare stood upright, steadying itself with one paw on the seat while it watched Roger and Viking approaching, then it went off with leisurely bounds from its long back legs. Roger knew that hares were magical, often spirits in disguise. He hoped it was not the magic leaving the Stones. He did not know if what they had once done they would do again, or if what he meant to do would offend whatever powers were in possession. He dismounted and did obeisance. He laid a branch of hawthorn in full flower before the Stones, for hawthorn was magic, too. He poured out the river water as a libation, as to the old gods. He made Viking kneel—a trick he had taught him after seeing the Midsummer Fair. Then he stood on the seat of the King Stone and persuaded Viking to put his two forefeet on it as well. He said out aloud,

"Permit us to go to Toby."

Viking put his feet back on the ground and Roger mounted him off the Stone and away they went, over land at once more open and more luxuriant, which did not puzzle him as much as it had done the first time. He cantered gently along through the common where the rabbits and fox cubs, the ducks resting on the riverbank, the otters playing, and the herons fishing took less notice of a horse passing by, even with a rider, than they would have done if Roger had been on foot. In the air there was such a wheeling and weaving of swallows at high speed that it was a wonder that Roger could canter through them without a collision. Sparrow hawks hovered motionless, regardless of the swallows, and partridges hurried their tiny young into cover. The world was teeming with life of every kind. Roger rejoiced in it, yet took it for granted. That was what his world had always been.

Among all these moving creatures he now saw in the distance one of his own kind, and recognized with a leap of his heart the incomparable chestnut with Toby riding. He galloped along to meet them hallooing at the top of his voice, which set all the animals scattering out of sight.

The boys pulled up side by side. Toby was less excited than Roger but courteous and friendly. His beautiful shining hair lifted in the breeze and he smiled as he said, "So it's you again, cousin. You did a fine vanishing trick last time. Or did you fall off that awkward big horse? I thought you were just behind me till I saw the empty saddle. And now I see that the saddle you are used to is a very different kind of thing."

"I did not fall off," said Roger indignantly. "You went without me as it happened. And my saddle is for

jousting. I wouldn't like to risk jousting on yours." Roger's saddle was wooden with a raised front to protect the rider where there could be no armor.

"*Jousting?* Do you mean to tell me there is somewhere in this country where they still do that? Where *do* you come from, cousin?"

"Here. I told you, but you wouldn't believe me. Never mind. Show me your horse's paces and I'll see if I can keep up."

"Right! A race. Where shall we go?"

Roger pointed back the way he had come.

"You see that little hill on the—" He was about to say, "on the edge of the forest," but turning round to face that way he saw that the forest had retreated beyond a landscape of rolling fields, so he finished, "on the skyline?"

"You mean Roger's Island?"

"Is that what it is called?" Roger's blood gave a leap through his veins. Could it be his name that had lasted so long?

"Yes. We will race there and jump the little stream."

"Do you go there often?" Roger was suddenly afraid his secret had been stolen.

"Sometimes we take a hamper there and eat. There's a fine view, and a pair of weird stones like children's seats. Linnet likes to sit on them."

Roger didn't mind Linnet. She was just the person. Besides, she had not been surprised at him! She had said he was one of *the others.* He wondered again who they were, and what they had in common.

"Ready?" said Toby. "Go!"

Away they went, the chestnut easily leading, skimming along like a bird while Toby's coattails flew behind him. But it was a long way and Viking though always behind was never tired. When they reached the little stream he was many lengths behind. The chestnut though sweating and heaving still managed to gather his pretty feet together and jump across, while Viking stopped dead, and after getting his breath back, dropped his head for a drink. He had never done any racing and had no thought of winning. Both boys laughed, as Roger pulled his horse's head up.

"He's a good one," said Toby. "I guess you haven't raced him much. Let's give him a second prize." He pulled off one of the ribbon bows that decorated his kneeband, crossed the plank-bridge, and tied the ribbon to Viking's bridle. "My Feste's a thoroughbred. King Charles is mad on racing, so we get quite a lot of practice round here. It's the fashion. Newmarket is rather far, but I have been there to watch. The King's always there when they race."

The mention of the King prompted Roger to ask a question that was troubling him.

"Doesn't the King speak French?"

"Well, yes. He must be able to, because he lived in France so long. And I suppose people at Court must because there are many visitors from France."

"Do you?"

Toby laughed. "Yes, but I expect it's as queer as your English."

"I speak French at home. Though my father is only half Norman the de Greys came over with the Conqueror."

"It's a long time to keep it up. Your people must be mad about the family tree," said Toby. "I know some old scholars at Cambridge who still talk in Latin. But English is the language for me."

"It sounds fine when you speak it."

Toby crossed over again. "Feste's sweating," he said, "I'll rub him down." He pulled up handfuls of dead grass and began to rub his horse's neck and shoulders. Viking now consented to jump the stream and the two horses blew in each other's nostrils. Roger dismounted and came round to take Viking's head in his hands and caress him in his sweetest English, glad to be able to speak it naturally into the right ears. Viking answered with a loving nicker and from Toby there came a gasp of laughing surprise. Roger looked round to see what had amused him, but there was no one there, neither boy nor horse nor any sight or sound of them going away. Roger laughed, too, rather bitterly, wishing he could share the joke with Toby. "Where is he?" he thought. "He must be here." Then he remembered. "It's not Toby who's done the vanishing trick, it's me again! It's always too short. Toby! Toby!" There was no answer. Five hundred and forty years is a long way for voices to travel.

Why had he not rushed back to the Stone and caught Toby up? Because the Stones were awesome and because his strict upbringing in manners to his elders had taught him to accept what was given and never ask for too much.

Roger rode home slowly, puzzled and truly lost in his thoughts. It seemed this shift in time could happen, but it was teasingly out of control. Here was Toby, the perfect companion, but to be with him was as difficult as holding water in your two hands.

Seven

The next day Osmund took Roger with him to visit Edgar at the Abbey, leading a packhorse carrying baskets of eels and eggs for the Abbot and honey and sweetmeats for Edgar. As they rode past the island hill, Roger noticed with pleasure how well the Stones were hidden.

"I see," said Osmund, "someone has been clearing back the scrub up there. It is a pity to let ground that has once been cleared go back into forest, but I don't know why it ever was cleared. It is an unprofitable piece. It's within our boundaries, I think. I must ask the steward who has been working there. It was a waste of time."

"I did it," said Roger. "I like it up there. It gives Viking an uphill gallop, and from the top you can see the whole of our lands. If it is of no use, I wish you would give it to me."

"Whatever for?"

"I like it. When I marry I'll build a house there."

Osmund laughed. "When you marry I'll give it to you. But your wife will want more than that."

Roger was content. It really would be called "Roger's Island."

It was while they were riding along the edge of the forest, mile after mile, and it still stretched before them, that Roger remembered that when he and Toby were racing toward it the forest had retreated to the horizon, and that its absence had hardly surprised him. There had been a landscape of fields and small coverts, looking so convincingly as if it had been there for ever that he had accepted it easily. Now he was shocked. The forest was very beautiful. The budding twigs of each tree were warm and burnished and the hawthorn and wild cherry in full flower. On the ground the sunlight lay in long streaks, falling in some places on an acre of bluebells, in another on the fronds of new bracken. They rode past a herd of black pigs who grunted and nosed contentedly under the trees while the swineherds lay on the grass. Farther on was a heavy wagon loaded with timber and drawn by oxen. How could people manage without a forest? It was as essential as water.

On the return journey as he neared home Roger was wondering how he could manage to be present when Linnet and her family decided to eat in the open air. He didn't like to be always haunting the house like an uninvited ghost. At the thought, he laughed. "Anyway, *it's my own house and I'm there all the time!*"

However, his next meeting was not planned by him at all. He had been kept busy by his father for three weeks, going to distant markets to buy fine cloth and presents for the lady Eleanor and the girls, or to pay visits at other manors whose lords they had met at the jousting. Roger also had to compete with Osmund's company of yeoman archers at their target practice. If there was any fighting for which they might be summoned by the earl, it would most likely be at this time of year. Bowmen were the infantry, whereas Roger when he grew up would be a knight and his weapons would be lance or sword. However, he practiced archery for hunting, though he would have to do it on horseback. He had heard of the fabulous archery of the Saracens, unerring at full gallop, and like all boys he longed to do similar feats or better.

It was late May before he found a chance to go privately to the Stones. The trees were now in full leaf, but they still had that vivid freshness of green which surprises winter eyes. Roger thought, can it ever really be as green as this? It is fantastic. It is too much. The whole air is green. The din from the birds is enough to make you put your hands over your ears, with the nightingales' long notes outdoing even the thrushes.

Roger sat by the Stones hugging his knees and looking at the spread of buttercups which covered the distant water meadows with sparkling yellow, first cousin of green.

He couldn't decide just what to do, but at last, overcome by the magic thrill of all this greenness, he took up his flageolet which he often carried in spring to imitate the birdsong, and began to play "Summer is Icumen in."

The notes took off and hung on the air—but they were somehow all twins. Roger played, and listened carefully to each note as it came out. The music overlapped, was one and the same.

He turned to look round, and there was Linnet sitting on the Queen Stone. A boy like Toby, but younger, was playing the flute. Toby had over his arm the bridles of two horses and a small black-and-white pony. Linnet stood up on the Stone and leapt up and down. "There he is! There's Roger. Look, Alexander, my Roger's come!"

Roger stopped playing to go to her, and at the same time Alexander put his flute down, and they all faded out. Roger took a gasping breath and played again, but in vain. He ran about with his arms

stretched out as if playing Blind Man's Buff, but they were gone.

"I'm always five hundred and forty years too soon," he shouted, but there was no answer.

He sat and thought with all his concentration and desire, but who can understand hard magic? Then suddenly out of the hopeless tangle of his thoughts it came into his mind that Linnet had been sitting on the Queen Stone. He had always sat on the other. What if the King looked forward but the Queen, like his mother and his grandmother, always looked back? He knew that on this occasion *he* had not moved in time. He was on his own ground. This time *they* were *the others.* As in his thoughts he used Linnet's expression, he realized what it meant. So Linnet and Toby knew "others" beside himself. Did someone else use the Stones?

What if Linnet, jumping up and down on the Stone, had perhaps accidentally, while she was thinking of him, come all the way back to him? But the others were there, too, and the horses. So then, perhaps the music, then and now together. There was certainly magic in that, but everyone knew music was magic. They did it in church.

He would have to find out if he was right about the Queen Stone. He jumped up to test his idea, but hesitated. How rash should he be? Linnet had come to him, but if *he* were to go back who knows what he might find? He was ashamed to be more nervous than Linnet—if indeed she had done it.

He dropped on one knee before the Queen Stone, then quietly took his place.

"Graciously grant me for one minute to go back five hundred and forty years..."

Terrified swarms of birds dashed past him escaping from the clang and rhythmical war cries away downriver, whence he heard shouting and dreadful screams like pig-sticking day. All the settlement was ablaze and the horizon billowing with smoke, but he could clearly see the long ships anchored in the river flying the Black Raven. Women and children ran in every direction while their men fought and were cut down with two-handed battle-axes. The boys that ran away were pursued and taken prisoner. It was impossible to recognize anyone at this distance, but the ground was strewn with the bodies of his men, the peasants of his own village. What about his family? The site of the manor was hidden in smoke and high flames taking off like birds. Roger's body had gone hot and cold with terror. They were surely all killed, his father in fighting, surprised without his armor. He must run and hide in the forest—and after, what should he do, alone? For a moment he covered his face with his hands and tears ran out between his fingers. But there was a robin close beside him singing its happy little conversation, undisturbed. Roger looked up.

The leaves rustled, the woodpeckers tapped, over all the wide landscape the sun blessed the growing wheat and the fat lambs. Watchet sat with an expression of idiotic bliss, his eyes closed, his nose twitching as the breeze brought something special to it. The only smoke was from the new chimney above the manor house roof.

Greatly upset, Roger realized that what he had seen was his grandmother's Saxon ancestors, taking over what was now his own, though it had come to him through the Normans conquering in their turn. And there had been Danish invasions since then, though not as far inland as here. If life went on like that, how could the manor house possibly last so long? But he knew that it had.

Eight

A great new interest had begun for Roger at home. It was eighteen months since any news had come from Bernard in Normandy. It was now known that the earl's brother whom he served as a page was a prisoner, his household scattered. This was not a reason to lose all hope. Letters had to be sent by hand, entrusted to chance travelers or merchants, risking the dangers of shipwreck or piracy at sea, and accident or robbery on land. The lady Eleanor, however, was worrying over her eldest son till she grew thin and ill. Osmund had thought of a plan to comfort her. An immense block of stone had been brought to the manor and set up against the side of the house by the entrance. A master sculptor was engaged to carve out a giant Saint Christopher, patron saint of travelers, to be invoked to bring Bernard safely home. Later on, when the saint should have done his work and brought

Bernard back, Osmund promised that he would build a chapel dedicated to him.

The sculptor lived in the new manor house while he was employed there. He was of course a workman and sat at the lower end of the common table, but he was highly respected. He was a small powerful man, silent and abstracted, but with flashes of humor that made all the pages laugh and caused those separated from him at the high table to ask what he had said.

The sculptor soon became an idol of Roger's who watched his every movement with wonder, whether he was sitting lost in thought or putting on his apron and setting out his tools. Roger was fascinated to watch him working, to see the chips flying and the shape coming. At first the figure was lumpier than a snowman, but Roger could see where the shoulder would be and which part would be a head. Then details grew out of the stone, a curl, a fold of drapery, an elbow. The next day the Christ child's head would be there and a little hand held up out of the stone as if out of water. For weeks Roger could hardly bear not to see it happening. It looked so easy. You hit in the right place just hard enough, and it came. The sculptor did not talk. He took no notice of questions. He whistled as a groom whistles, to keep the dust out of his mouth.

It was early autumn before Roger went to the Stones again. So much had happened in between that, though he had not forgotten, he was willing to postpone further experiments. As for the Queen Stone, that adventure had frightened him badly. He did not wish to try again, but he hoped Linnet would, to find him. He paid his respects to the King and took his place there. How far should he go? He had been lucky with the dandelion result the first time. What could have been better than to find Linnet, Toby, and Alexander? He would leave it to chance again. He picked another dandelion seedhead.

"We got to the year sixteen hundred and sixty. How much further shall I go?" As he drew in his breath to blow, a sudden gust of wind came to his assistance and took off all the head but one thread like a white hair. It took four puffs to move it. "One hundred and forty." Roger made a rapid calculation.

"If it please you, I wish to visit Green Knowe in the year of Our Lord eighteen hundred." When he had said it he winced at the thought of what he had done. Eighteen hundred! The end of the world might have happened before then. It might be the Day of Judgement!

The world fortunately looked all right, very much as he had seen it on his former forward flight, except that the tracks had become lanes and even roads, of a width and surface that surprised him. As he drew near the village, of which every house however small had a chimney, he saw passing along the road, above the lines of bushes that screened it on either side, the bobbing heads of horsemen or the perched-up driver of some kind of wheeled chariot going at a brisk trot and almost silently. He would have liked to see these near to, but the road swung away from the direct line to the manor house and disappeared behind trees.

The house itself also was hidden from him by trees of which a great number had sprung up in all these hedgerows. To Roger, a descendant of men who had laboriously cleared from the endless forest enough land to live on, it seemed very wasteful. But of that demon-haunted forest there seemed nothing left. He approached as before through the wood where he had first seen Linnet, which now had a well-used footpath through it. Once out of this he would see the house and all its outbuildings.

One step more, and Roger cried out in grief. The house had gone! Gone altogether, and instead of it there was a square red building much bigger, with many chimneys. It stood where his own house had stood, with eight-foot-high windows upstairs and down, looking over smooth grass where the moat should have been. He had watched the moat being dug out. What a work it had been! And now someone had filled it up

again. He did not admire the house. It looked flimsy to him. Any siege catapult would knock it down in no time, and without the moat it had no defense against war boats rowing up the river.

There seemed, surprisingly, no one about as he walked cautiously up to take a look. He found that the walls were made of blocks of what felt to the touch like coarse earthenware. "A house made like a jug!" he thought contemptuously. He looked through the windows. They were made of solid air—you could rap on it with a fingernail! He had heard the builders speak of glass in cathedrals and palaces but never imagined it as like this. They had said it kept the cold out, but most of the light as well, being thick and colored and set in a network of lead.

Roger could see inside the room. It was filled with fragile-looking seats that would hardly bear a man. Their twiggy legs were painted with, he supposed, gold leaf such as monks use in their holy books. Tiny tables were scattered about beside them, and in one corner stood an immense gold harp, such as no minstrel could carry. This room must be for a royal family. Perhaps the earl's descendants had seized the throne and this was one of their summer palaces. Over the floor was spread a rich material. Crusaders returning from the East had told of such things in Constantinople, but Roger had never seen one. Most wonderful of all, over the fireplace was a carved gold frame, about the height of a man, in which the whole view of the garden and river outside was repeated, with the window frame and himself looking in. He knew it was himself because it waved its arms when he did. Frightening magic! It was like the reflection in still water, but it couldn't be water standing on end like that. Or like his mother's metal hand mirror but much clearer. It must be a huge sheet of highly polished metal—silver surely. He watched the swallows weaving about in it and a pair of swans flying past, and the first autumn leaves flickering down. Certainly that, if not magic, was fascinating. Otherwise the room seemed to him flimsy and silly, even for a queen's room. He felt angry when he thought of the strong simplicity that it had replaced. Alas! That had not lasted till now. Why should anyone pull down such a strong thing? It could have lasted a long time yet. He grieved as for a friend killed in battle treacherously.

Roger moved dejectedly round the side of the tall red building and found himself in what he supposed must be the queen's garden. There was closely scythed grass and beds of flowers, surrounded by a ring of big trees whose branches swept the ground. That circular line was once the edge of the moat. He crossed the grass openly. After all, this was his ground, though that would be hard to explain to any of the king's guards who might be about. He passed under the trees, and to his great delight saw that at least this part of the moat was still there, still full of water, with moorhens and ducks on it. But what he thought of as "the real moat at home" had no trees. It was kept clear and was stockaded.

Roger walked along the bank and presently came to a big tree whose purple and vermilion leaves hung like a vast silken tent all round it. He stepped into the great space underneath, which was lit by a thousand dancing specks of light where the sun glanced between overlapping leaves. He could never have imagined such a beautiful domed palace—an Eastern palace such as he had heard of, all colored and yet dusky. He gasped as he looked up and round, and saw that he was not alone.

Sitting on the ground near the trunk was a young girl, prettily dressed but carelessly rumpled, and beside her a black boy. They seemed very happy together. Roger had occasionally seen black men in the crews of foreign trading ships. This was clearly a princess and her attendant, though they behaved more like sister and brother. She looked at Roger with the keen attention of a startled deer.

"Who's there, Jacob? Is it Tolly?"

The black boy answered, "Don't see no one, Missy."

"You always say that! What's the good of having eyes if you don't see? Is that you, Tolly?"

"Forgive me if I startled you, lady. My name is Roger d'Aulneaux. I came looking for a very old house, but it has gone."

"There, you see, Jacob," she said. "He's one of *the others*." Then turning to Roger, "You have the right name, only the "d" has got in the wrong place. I'm Susan. Come and sit by me here. Do you know Tolly? I felt sure it was he."

"Is he one of *the others*? I don't know him yet. Do you know Linnet?"

"Oh yes! I often hear her laughing. She loves it here. She'll never go away. Tolly knows her, and Toby and Alexander."

"Me know Feste," said the black boy. "Jacob understand animals very well. Feste is horse for Great God Holy Spirit."

Roger laughed. "You're right," he said. "I want to meet Tolly. Does he live here?"

"They all live here," said Susan, "only it's very chancy. It's like whether a raindrop is going to splash on your face or it isn't. It just happens."

"Doesn't it make any difference to Toby and the others that it's gone?"

"What's gone?"

"The house they used to live in."

"But it's not gone. It's not gone, it's only hiding. I wish I could see it, but I know the feel of it. It's there inside."

"Missy see nothing," Jacob explained, "but she know very much." Then Roger looked again at Susan and understood that she was blind.

"Push branches aside and see."

Roger did as Jacob said, and sure enough from here he could see the rear of the building. Out of a high red mansion that dwarfed it, there stuck out, like an oversized porch, the front gable of his own stone house with its Norman window, its stone steps and the entrance on the upper floor, weather-worn but still obdurate. Beside the entrance stood Saint Christopher, looking nearly as old as the Stones and like them when Roger discovered them, half covered with ivy and traveler's joy; Saint Christopher who in other time was not yet finished. Roger's eyes filled with tears as he realized how dear these things were that had endured.

As he looked he tried to puzzle out what had happened. Could they have pulled down the rest of those immensely solid walls, or would they have left them inside and built that flimsy red stuff as an outside curtain? He longed to run up the stairs and look in on his own hall. Why not? But as he stepped forward

Susan called, "Can you see it?" Her voice was a little sad, for she could never see it.

"Yes. There's somebody watching out of a top window."

"That will be Caxton. He won't see you. He never sees *the others*. My mama hates the old house. She is always urging Papa to knock it down. She calls it his old-fashioned folly because follies are the height of fashion but they are supposed to be Gothic, not Norman. And anyway we have got a ruined chapel. She says the Norman house is a relic of barbarism and makes her ashamed whenever she has visitors. But my papa loves it. He won't have it touched. And I love it, too. Mama has given it to me for my day room, because she says as I can't see it doesn't make any difference to me. But I know the old part as if it were alive. The sun warm on stone is quite different from the sun on wood, though the old floor is lovely, too, but brick doesn't give anything back. And the stone room has faint echoes as if it was thinking. But you have to be alone in it for that."

"I'm almost never alone in it," said Roger, "but when I play my flageolet, it's as if it was waiting for someone. Alexander perhaps."

He let the branches of the beech tree swing back into place to shut out the big red house that he did not want to see. Once again the three children were enclosed in a breathing dome of pheasant-coloured leaves.

"Wouldn't this be the very place for us all to meet?" he said.

"Yes," answered Susan, listening to the wide circle of the tree whispering round her. "We could give a party here, if we knew how to invite them. Jacob is wonderfully clever about everything else. I expect he could get Feste and Toby's deer and Orlando, Tolly's dog, but he is slow about *the others*. I suppose it's because he wasn't born here. But he shares a sea shanty with Tolly. Sometimes they answer each other from the top of different trees, like birds. Alexander talks with birds, too. He does a lovely nightingale. Whenever I hear one, I wonder if it's Alexander. Sometimes I wonder if the birds have something to do with it. They have gone on through all time telling us the same thing."

There was the sound of footsteps approaching and voices, and somewhere a gardener suddenly started vigorously working. Roger heard a man's low sentimental voice and in answer a cooing laugh that was at once silly, caressing, and cruel.

"That's Mama," said Susan. "She spoils everything."

Roger, with that reeling feeling that he was getting to know, sat on the Stone with his head in his hands, and picked leaves like pheasant's feathers out of his hair. He put them in his wallet. Linnet's prim-roses had long since faded, but Viking still wore Toby's ribbons on his bridle.

There was much to think of as he trotted home-ward. He had imagined the house besieged by ene-mies in some new war, or struck by a thunderbolt and burnt out, but never as being threatened by a vain woman just wanting something newer. Of course his house was new, the very newest thing, but it was meant to last, not like that palace made of blocks of baked mud. Even if it had glass windows, they were no protection against enemies. But then, there is no protection either against a silly woman. She will go on and on till she gets what she wants.

This was a depressing thought. When he got home, Roger went into the storeroom on the ground floor to look at the wooden pillar on which he had put his lucky sign. There were five more pillars so he carved it on each, getting better at it as he went on. He knew from Olaf that the tree of heaven was an ash called Yggdrasil. All these timbers were oak, but he hoped the sign would work. He remembered that there was a holy sign on the stonework upstairs, and was a little comforted. After all, the house was still there in that far time, though partly hidden.

He went to look for his grandmother. She was the easiest person to talk to. She seemed to be too old to have any wishes or passions of her own. When other people were fretful or indignant she only laughed and said, "What a fuss!" And she never repeated what was said to her.

Roger found her sitting in the window seat in the last afternoon sun. He leaned against her with his elbows on her knees.

"What's troubling you, my grandson?"

"What can be done with a silly woman?"

"What a grown-up question! You're not thinking of marrying one?"

"I don't mean to. But it seems that quite sensible people do. And a woman can spoil everything. This house, for instance."

"When you marry you must take my advice. I won't let you take a silly one. And then it will be all right."

"But Grandmother, there's a lot of time after me."

"Yes. A lot of time after, and before."

He looked at her with sudden understanding. "Yours was all before," he said. "You had many children, didn't you?"

"Twelve. But only seven of them lived to grow up."

"Where do you think the others are?"

"Why, with me, of course. Where else should the little dears be? They didn't know anywhere else."

"What about heaven?"

"They can wait for me. We are all together."

"Do you ever see them?"

"No. I hear them, and at night I sometimes feel a warm head with very soft hair, on my shoulder."

Roger kissed her and went away feeling everything was really quite natural.

He looked with new eyes at the circle of the moat. It was quite bare of trees on both sides, nowhere for an enemy to take cover, and well stockaded. The wide space within it contained, besides the house, the Saxon hall, the kitchens, the dairy, the barn, the farmyard, the pump and well, the carpenter's shop and various sheds. It was the busy heart of the estate, self-contained in case of invasion. There was only a small trellised enclosure where his mother and sisters sat in fine weather. How strange that it should have become instead the heart of idleness, heavy with trees and the scent of flowers, and in the center of it a dream tree.

The problem now was to find Tolly. Where in the seven hundred years was he to be looked for? Or perhaps he was still further in the future? Roger's thoughts were on him as he waited at table, offering the bowl of water for hand-washing or the carved meat first to his father, going down on one knee as was only proper. Etiquette did not oblige him to kneel to the ladies, but he did so this time to his grandmother.

Osmund smiled at him, but his sisters laughed and said, "What's come over Roger? He's very reverent today."

"I shan't be to you," he answered, kneeling elegantly to his mother so as not to leave her out. To the girls he offered the dishes with a chilly indifference and afterward walked away with an exaggeratedly courtly air that made everyone laugh.

After supper, when the great peach-colored autumn moon was rising, and outside the house the swifts were screaming as they swooped on evening gnats, their screams drawn past the windows like curved lightning, Roger played on his flageolet and listened carefully. The stone walls received the sound and seemed to give back something more, as if they made an assertion. "Alexander, can you hear me?" he asked silently but urgently. But there was a burst of laughter in the hall. Everyone was talking. The pages were playing marbles, and as their "blood alleys" ran along the wooden floor with little jumps as a marble crossed from one board to the next, the walls received that sound also. Could Jacob play marbles with Susan? In this room, too, it would be. Why had he not looked in? Could you play marbles by ear? Perhaps if Jacob tapped where the marble was that Susan must aim at, she would. Her ears were very keen. "Susan, can you hear me?" Did someone answer "course"?

Nine

The Stones were the sort of things that any boy was sure to find if he roamed the country. Roger had found them, and the Oldknow children had found them. Jacob, he guessed, had not because he would seldom leave Susan. Perhaps Tolly had. Roger set off with Watchet to try his luck.

It was a wild windy day. The air was full of thousands of birds gathering to fly off who knows where. They swirled in black clouds over the open land, blown this way and that by the wind. The rooks above the rookery were playing with the wind like boys on ice. They shot downwind and then staggered up, calling and challenging. Scores of wood pigeons foraged in the stubble where the corn had been cut, watched by several young foxes with an eye to dinner.

There was such a commotion going on in the sky with racing clouds, the sun coming and going and hawks wheeling, that Roger was head-in-air as he climbed the hill to the Stones. Watchet, as always, rushed to his old rabbit hole to see if anything was there. He drew back, wagging and puzzled, as a rough-haired black-and-white body with a short tail backed out. A small whiskery face covered with soil looked round at him, barked, and went in again. This was a kind of dog Roger had never seen. He supposed it was a dog because it was nothing else and it behaved like one. He was surprised that Watchet did not attack it, but on the contrary, sniffed it and wagged.

"That's Orlando," said a voice. Roger whipped round and saw a boy just getting up from the Queen Stone. He was dressed in tight trousers of something like blue linen but very faded and patched in different colours, and a ridiculously short woollen tunic that only just covered his waist, and he wore sandals. His clothes in fact were much the same sort of thing as his own, but to Roger's eyes very poor and skimpy.

"Are you with the woodcutters?" he asked.

"No," the boy answered, "I come from the house down there." He pointed in the direction of Green Knowe. "Where do you live?"

Roger grinned all over his face. "I'll give you one guess," he said.

"London? I don't know where else you could have got those smashing clothes. Just look at your leather belt! It's terrific."

"It was made here, by the saddler, and the buckle by Olaf Olafson."

"Swank!" said the boy with the most friendly grin. "I wish I had one." The boys had to shout to make themselves heard against the wind. "I say, are we allowed in this wood? You can't see it from the manor. I didn't know it was there. I suppose none of the roads run beside it. It looks terribly private and special. More like something in Grimms' fairy tales, not at all trodden and tamed."

"Tamed! I should think not! We are all in fear of it. The swineherds go a little way in, and the woodcutters have their working tracks, but if you lose sight of those you are done for, unless you can see the sun which generally you can't. And it isn't only wolves. There are often bands of murderers or outlaws in hiding. We never go beyond the fringe."

"But it's broad daylight now. Couldn't we go through it together? Do you know where we would come out?"

"We wouldn't come out. It goes on forever. That's where the demons come in."

"Go on! There isn't such a forest in England."

Roger laughed. "I believe you don't really know where you are," he said. "Look here, have you ever seen leaves like that?" He brought out his pheasant-back leaves.

"Why yes, of course I have. There's a copper beech in our garden. It's gorgeous. People say it is the best in all England."

"These leaves came from it. I was there yesterday—though that's not quite the right word."

"I didn't see you."

"I expect we weren't there at the same time. You're Tolly of course—I'm Roger. Now listen. You were sitting on that stone there. You need to be very careful what you think when you sit on it. What were you wishing?"

"I was wishing I could see the first boy that ever lived in the manor, I guess it would be about eight hundred and fifty years ago."

"That's me, Roger d'Aulneaux, and I was looking for you as it happens."

"It can't be you. You look just like now."

"It is now, for me at any rate." They looked at each other and laughed. They really were very much alike.

"Roger d'Aulneaux," he repeated, "living in the newly built manor house. Since you have told me where *you* are in time, I'll come and look for you under the beech tree tomorrow. We never get more than a tantalizing snatch of time. You'll need a proof."

"I don't understand a word you say. Proof of what?"

"Of the forest. Come, we'll go in. We can follow

the stream and that will show us the way back. Many boys have gone in and never come out again."

Roger led the way. The leaves were coloring but had hardly begun to fall. Those that fled on the wind had been violently torn off, and those on the trees flapped like little pennons on knights' lances. The trees gradually grew closer together and before long the boys entered the forest proper. The little stream lost its sparkle and flowed sullenly in darkness. The trunks were crowded, their branches tangled and interlacing. The ground was soft from centuries of fallen leaves and the wind that had been so gay and rough outside did not stir the rich smell of mold, of endless growing and decaying that enclosed the boys, and while from the tops of the trees there came a sound like surf where the wind streamed through them, this was heard as a noise outside when one is indoors. Among the trunks there was a silence that could be recognized as spreading as far all round as could be imagined. Whichever way the boys looked the trunks rose up and shut out the horizon. Here and there was a little dell with a giant tree in the center, where a shower of broken light came down. These glades were recognizable, but it was impossible to tell in which direction one had crossed them last time, so they were not helpful landmarks.

There was no birdsong, it being autumn, but occasionally the uncanny voice of a young owl and the rustling of unseen creatures. There was so strong a feeling of isolation, of silence, of secrecy and supernatural power (for trees are alive—they have a still, rooted, powerful life), such a sense of having been there since the beginning, that Roger was cut to the heart by his knowledge that in the future it would not be there. While he felt with all his senses the unconquerable presence of the forest and the awe of it that he had grown up with, he could not believe it could disappear. It was in its essence everlasting. And yet this would vanish and his father's house, robbed of its tremendous neighbor, would stand.

"You'll want a proof," Roger repeated. "Wait a minute."

While Tolly sat by the stream, now so small as to be almost invisible under grass and ferns, where Watchet and Orlando were wading about sniffing for water rats, Roger cut off a branch of yew. He peeled off the bark revealing rose-pink wood. He whittled it down to a medallion, on which he engraved the ash-seed pattern that was on his knife.

"You can bore a hole and wear it," he said offering it to Tolly. "It's a charm."

Tolly was fingering it with surprise and wonderment when, at a distance impossible to place, there rose in the air a high inhuman wail. Watchet stiffened with every hair on end.

"Help!" said Tolly picking up Orlando. "What was that?"

"A young wolf. It's the season for them. You can guess, more or less, what an old one will do, but the young ones are tricky. We'd better get back. The sun must be nearly down."

"I've got a knife," said Tolly stoutly, "though it's not as good as yours. How far away do you think it was?"

"No telling. And they travel fast. But we've got Watchet. He's good."

The boys set off at a run with their dogs close at heel. They stopped at intervals to take breath and listen, hoping to hear that ghostly sound still at a distance, but there was no sound at all, so the wolf might be anywhere, and not only one.

"I see what you mean," said Tolly panting. "Without the stream I shouldn't have a clue where to go. Come on." He stumbled forward and a large body sprang up out of the bracken at his feet; not a wolf lying in wait, but a deer that bounded away.

"Good," said Roger, "that will be more to their liking than us. Let them chase that."

Watchet had been trained not to chase deer, which belonged to the king, but Orlando was careering madly through the forest yelling as he went.

"We'll have to leave him. He's determined to get himself eaten."

"I can't leave Orlando." Tolly took a small metal thing out of his pocket and blew down it. No sound came, but from a distance Orlando returned with heaving sides and what looked like a double length of tongue. Roger was dumbfounded.

"What is that you have got?"

"It's a whistle. It makes a note humans can't hear but dogs can."

"Who made it for you?" asked Roger thinking of Olaf Olafson and his magic.

"Why, nobody. You can buy them anywhere. I'd better carry this little fool." He picked up Orlando and they set off again. The light was fading rapidly. The general color of the crowded trunks was a dusty purple-green like grapes. The forest seemed now and again to give great sighs as if it had just woken up. There was much more rustling, of day creatures taking cover and night creatures coming out.

"I shall be glad when we get out," said Tolly. "Humans don't seem to be expected here, or wanted. It's almost as though they hadn't happened yet. Thank goodness, I can see sky between the trunks."

As the boys came near the edge of the forest, from farther up came a great hullabaloo and a herd of black pigs rushed out onto the track, followed by

three swineherds and their dogs. Roger waved to the boys, whom he knew. They came from the Abbey, and went off that way, their pigs squealing ahead of them.

A little later as Roger and Tolly were coming out, a string of six foxes trotted through the trees ahead of them and out into the open land.

"Halloo-loo-loo-loo," shouted Roger as Watchet and Orlando streaked after them.

"Come up to the Stones, Tolly. We can watch the chase from there. You can see for miles." They crossed the plank and ran up the slope, tired but excited by freedom after anxiety. Tolly sat on the Queen Stone to watch, but Roger, after the enclosed air of the forest, found the rollicking wind exhilarating. The crimson rim of the sun was just disappearing and across the pinkish clouds myriads of birds were homing to roost, black swarms of starlings swirled like smoke, herons slowly flapping, hundreds of rooks all flying separately but calling to each other as they went, a cloud of goldfinches blown about by the wind as if they were merely feathers yet managing to keep closely together, flocks of pigeons in perfect array, their wings beating in time; a wonderful pageant of homecomings.

Roger stood watching the chase. The foxes had scattered, and the two dogs chased first one and then another, crisscrossing like mad things over the land. He had good eyesight and it was easy to follow the ridiculous little black-and-white bundle of enthusiasm that was Orlando, but presently he saw that only Watchet was still pursuing. He couldn't see Orlando anywhere.

"Blow your magic whistle," he said, turning round to Tolly. There was no one there.

The Stones were standing there alone with long feelers from the sun painting them royal crimson for a brief moment before all color faded out; then they took on their mysterious, remembering, twilight look.

Ten

At home the lady Eleanor was going through the stock of linen to see what needed to be woven in the winter. She smiled as he came in.

"What a wanderer you have become."

Roger kissed her hand. "But I'll always come home, always." He leaned against the wall and passed his hands over the stone. "And this will always be here. I wish the d'Aulneaux arms were carved somewhere. Couldn't you persuade Father to have them done over the fireplace?"

"It would look well," she said, "but Saint Christopher is not finished yet. I will talk to your father, while the sculptor is here."

"Because the house has a long future and I would like my name on it."

"*Your* name! You are not the only one."

"I know. But I think I mind most."

"Dear boy," said his grandmother from the fireside, "things get broken and *lost*, even great houses."

"But not this one." Then Roger remembered how for a minute he had thought it had altogether gone, and he added, "It may go into hiding."

The lady Eleanor said, "What nonsense!" but his grandmother agreed.

"That can happen," she said, "if someone built something bigger all round it."

"How did you know that?" Roger asked without thinking.

"It happens," she said, "even with birds' nests and most of all with palaces."

"This is neither one nor the other," said Roger obstinately. But he wondered uneasily what sort of a house Tolly lived in. What if Susan's horrid mother had had her way? Dare he go and see? If the house wasn't there he thought his heart would stop beating.

Of course he had to go. Eight hundred and fifty years back Tolly had come to him, so he must go eight hundred and fifty years forward. Far as he had gone into the future, except that each time more land was cultivated and new ways of building and dressing had come in, there had been nothing totally strange to him, nothing beyond his comprehension. He had noticed in the yard the old pump still in use, though the wooden handle had been replaced by iron. He had seen men scything in the fields, but had been surprised, it is true, to see powerful horses ploughing instead of oxen; men traveled on horseback, or they walked, which did not surprise him at all; and they cut trees down with axes, as you would expect. What had interested him very much was the light-running horse-drawn carriage that he had heard but not seen. Also, it was reassuring that Tolly was so like him, and had mistaken him for a contemporary, so that it was without misgiving that he launched himself into the future again to keep his appointment under the beech tree.

When he rose from the Stone, the first thing he noticed was the stale dead air, with a general smell that he didn't know. He had a quick nose that gave him instant warning. The forest of course was not there, so rich in its own smell. It was now a mass of houses starting only a few fields away from him. He turned quickly away from something too unbelievable to be taken in. He faced the view of the river and his own land. The wide watermeadows were untouched on both sides of the river, but beyond them were houses again, not as in a city huddled together in narrow busy streets, smoky from a thousand wood fires, like Cambridge, but wastefully scattered everywhere, each house separate, and most of them without either roof-vent or chimney. Roger was staggered. Where did all these people come from, and what did they live on? How could the land provide food for them? No wonder they had no chimneys, for without a forest what would they burn?

The way to Green Knowe was still across pasture and stubble, but the track to the Abbey had become what seemed to Roger an important road. There was nothing on it, which did not surprise him as the shiny surface was most unsuitable for horses, though good for wagons and oxen. He would not like to ride Viking far on it. He crossed it and took to the fields again, making toward the river. After a while he began to wonder what it was that made him feel so desolate, till he realized that except for the cows he had not seen an animal and hardly a bird. There were no horses, no donkeys, no rabbits nor hares. No partridges rose up under his feet, no foxes were prowling, no wagtails running about, no ducks on the river, no herons, no swarms of goldfinches over the thistles, no heavy bumblebees, and no butterflies. Consequently there was an unnaturally still dead air—he heard no rabbit-thudding, no small wings purring or large wings flapping, no quacking and splashing, no harsh cry from the heron, no tinkling sound, like Linnet's bracelets, from the goldfinches, no bumbling, no soft beat of butterflies' wings past his ear. There was only an occasional rook talking to itself in a melancholy way as it went over, and there were two swans on the river and a moorhen, and in the fields a few starlings. The world seemed nearly dead. Could there have been a dreadful plague that had killed the lovely worldful? For there were no wild flowers either, except ragwort. Where were the rushes, the rose-bay, the water irises, the waterlilies, the loosestrife, the campion, clover, and heartsease? He was walking along a hedge between two flowerless and lifeless fields when he heard, or rather felt before he heard it, an ear-tearing screech, as over him shot a giant bird which swooped up into the sky. Roger in terror had taken cover flat under the hedge with the instinct of any mouse when the owl hoots. If there were things like that about, no wonder there were no animals left. And yet the cows did not stampede. They didn't even open their eyes as they chewed the cud. Roger was getting to his feet when another of these horrors came, and then two more. The whole sky was full of their noise, but in a very short time they were out of sight and sound. Roger dared to get up again and go on his way, even more astonished than afraid. They were truly terrifying, but also awe-inspiring and exhilarating, as startled fear so often is. Their shape was not like any bird he knew, but it was the shape of speed itself, and their power was such that he could think of nothing to compare with it. Again he thought of Viking. He would certainly have gone mad and bolted and probably broken his neck.

Roger ran across the fields, pausing by each hedge as he came to it to look and listen. There was a continual hum in the air that seemed to pulse, that grew louder as he went on. Perhaps the sails of a windmill in a high wind was the sound nearest to it, or a waterwheel in spate heard inside the mill when the machines are turning.

When he had crossed the site of the old ferry by a new bridge he found himself for the first time in among the houses, and this made him uncomfortable like a dog in a strange yard. In his village everyone knew everyone, and in a neighbouring village from the kind of house you could guess what the owner was. He could not imagine what kind of people lived in these boxes or how they would treat him, or how he should address them. Obviously they were not work-men. They could not be knights because nowhere could he see stables or horses. Yet the funny thing was, there was no one about.

Almost at once he found himself beside a road three times as big as the one to the Abbey, smooth and silvery and going straight out of sight in both directions. Along this road, faster than a deer can run, as fast as an arrow can fly, went things like giant beetles on wheels. They droned like cockchafers as they approached, screaming as they went past him as a swift passes, and followed by roars and stinking fumes. Roger clutched himself into the hedge, peering like a squirrel, but as they went endlessly past and seemed tied to the road, he grew less frightened and more curious, and at last stood out to watch. He soon saw that there were people in them. To what emergency could they be going so fast, or from what danger fleeing? Was this why there seemed no one in the houses? He was standing there dazed when one with flashing lights and a noise like gravel falling out of a cart crunched to a halt beside him. A hand opened a door in the side and beckoned. Roger turned and ran for his life back to the river bank, where he felt safer because it was, though sadly changed, still familiar.

Very much shaken he went along the bank. Everywhere were scraps of unknown materials lying about, trodden into the mud; bits of silver beaten out like illuminator's silver leaf but crumpled and thrown away, and small squares as thin as skin and as transparent as water, but tough as leather. They all had lettering on them. He thought they must be messages to be sent by arrow. There were metal containers that would surely be useful, though he cut his hand on one. He even found a glass bottle with a clever metal top—a real treasure, a rarity worth any money. His mother's greatest treasure was a tiny blue vial for scent. This was much bigger. He put it in the wallet at his belt. Had they all been running for their lives and dropping things as they went? There were big black bales of things dumped by the side of the path.

Roger felt quite lost. Nothing was left of his lands or his life as he knew it. What should he find instead of his proud old house? It was like a nightmare from which he longed to wake up. To keep his spirits up he thought of Tolly, who had not seemed at all frightened or worried and had mistaken him for someone "now."

He came at last to the little wood where he had first seen Linnet, and now the roar of those dragon-beetles was turning away and growing less. The wood was still there, but only just. It had dwindled to a few small trees and several fallen trunks of once huge elms, but he greeted it like an old friend who has lost everything but is pitied and loved. On the other hand, so many trees had grown up round the manor house that he had to go some way beyond the wood, with growing apprehension before he could see it, but then his astonishment was like a shout of joy. The old house was there, complete with its steep tiled roof, its high-gabled ends, its stone windows that he had taken such pride in when they were being built. He

looked at it as if he had not seen it for a whole life-
time. The square red building was what had van-
ished, only one wall was left, with its big windows.
These now looked out into a garden such as Roger
had never seen or heard of, with bushes cut into the
shape of crowns or the orb and cross. The king must
surely stay here. Roger had never asked Susan if she
was a princess. Nevertheless he now felt confident
again. This was his house, his land where surely he
had a right to be, where he was coming to meet others who also were there by right, loving it as he did.
He forgot the nightmares he had had on the way here.
This was Green Knowe.

As soon as he entered the little gate from the river
bank his lungs were filled with the old scent of sweet
briar and honeysuckle and yew, and lush tangled
growing. Every bush rustled with birds. Above the
borders of flowers butterflies undulated like the
petals taking off. Their air was full of swallows gathering for their autumn flight, twittering with excitement. White doves and blue pigeons rocked in the
tops of trees, squirrels ran along the roof and took
wild leaps onto the nearest branches, swinging like
acrobats. Robins sang and blackbirds postured and
fought.

There seemed to be no one about except an old
gardener clipping the bushes with shears. He had

thought it was a man, but as he came nearer he saw it was an old woman—surely—not his grandmother? So very like her but in breeches and an apron!

"Grandmother!" he said. "How did you get here?"

"Through the front door, you goose. Who are you pretending to be?" she answered laughing. "But my dear Tolly! Where did you get those clothes? I know there's been a jumble sale, but those are London's best. And the gold torque round your neck. It's a marvelous reproduction. It looks just like real gold. And yesterday you came back with a strange amulet. I took it to the Archaeological Museum while you were out and they said it was Scandinavian and possibly a thousand years old. Now what are you laughing at? I know that look."

"You're not my grandmother. You're Tolly's. And I'm not Tolly. I'm Roger."

"Bless my soul! My dear boy! I believe you are a real Norman, and exactly like Tolly."

Roger grinned impishly. "Not so real today," he said. "I had my turn yesterday. Is Tolly under the beech tree?"

"He's been there all day. I wondered why. Be off to him then."

Roger went round the side of the house, birds flying before him. The upstairs seemed unchanged, but there were big windows all round on the ground floor.

He peered in and saw the walls of his old store-room, stone and plaster just as before, and an arrow-slit window, but there were no wooden pillars down the center. Instead there was a fireplace even bigger than the one upstairs, with a chimney going up through the middle of the house. There were brightly patterned curtains and great cushioned chairs big enough to go to bed in. One huge thick cloth covered what had been the mud floor, and on it stood a long table with candles. It looked a festive room. He could imagine them all, Toby, Alexander, Linnet, Susan, Tolly, and himself sitting down to a feast, with Jacob as page and the grandmother at the head. This was a good change. He approved. On the far side of the house the big trees clustered round, their branches almost sweeping the walls, but among them the old house stood, freed from all additions. Only the outside stairs were missing. It was worn and crumbly, crooked and weathered and gentle, like the two grandmothers, but truly itself still. "O my house," he thought. "Live forever!"

In the trees two thrushes were repeating to each other their touching autumn song, remembering the summer that had gone and hoping for the next. Altogether at peace, Roger moved aside the beech branches and went underneath. There was a light breeze that stirred the pavilion of leaves so that the

boughs drooping down to the ground, and the ground itself, and the children there, were all jeweled with shifting specks of light. Tolly, with Orlando, was lying on the soft ivy and moss beside Susan, to whom he was showing his amulet and telling her about a very great forest with wolves. With her finger she was tracing the ash-seed pattern.

"Oh," she said, "I know this pattern. You know the old shed along one side of the yard? Well, it has very worm-eaten old wooden posts to hold the roof up, and they have all got this pattern on them. I've often felt it and wondered."

"So that's where they are now," said Roger. "I carved those patterns on them as soon as the house was built, to bring it luck."

"This is Roger," said Tolly.

"I know," said Susan smiling at him.

"Where's Jacob?" Roger asked.

"Oh, poor Jacob. You know he can't always do it. Jacob! Jacob! Sing your sea shanty, Tolly."

Tolly sang, *"A-sailing down along the coast of high Barbary."*

In reply a voice, very loud and full for a boy, answered with a few notes from the height above them, and while squirrels scattered in all directions along their branch roads, there was a slithering twiggy sound and Jacob came looping down from bough to bough and dropped beside Susan.

"Jacob here, Missy." Orlando sprang to him and wagged a special welcome.

"Well done," said Susan. "That makes four of us."

"If I'd brought my flageolet," said Roger, "I might have been able to find Alexander. We share a tune, too."

"I've been here all the time," said Alexander, who was sitting in the undergrowth speckled all over with dancing lights so that he was very nearly invisible. "I've been having a flute conversation with a thrush."

"That makes five."

A voice outside in the open said, "Come on, Toby, Alexander's under the beech tree, I heard him imitating the thrush." The leaves were lifted and Linnet, nursing a leveret, came in followed by Toby leading a beautiful fallow deer with a jeweled collar.

"Oh," said Linnet, "here's my Roger again. How alike he and Tolly are! At first I thought it was the same boy, but Roger looks fiercer."

"The grandmother thought I was Tolly."

"Oh well," said Tolly, "she gets mixed up. She often calls me Toby."

"Six, seven," said Susan. "Who's 'real' today?"

"It's Tolly today," said Roger.

The curtain was parted yet again, and this time a tall slim girl came in. She was the same age as Toby and just as beautiful, with long shining hair. She hesitated just inside the circle, like someone who is lonely.

"May I come in?" she said. "I was thinking of you all and couldn't bear to be left out. It was my beech tree, too."

"That makes eight," said Susan. "Who is it?"

"It's me, you know."

Tolly laughed and ran across to her.

"I know you," he said, taking her hand. "I'd know you anywhere, any time. You're my grandmother. There's only one of you."

"Dear Tolly! I've always lived here you know. I've seen and heard them all often."

"We know you, too," they said. Susan got up and came to take her arm. "I wish you had been my grandmother. Mine was horrid."

"She old crocodile," said Jacob. "Old snapper. She beat Missy with walking stick. She not stay here."

The young grandmother-to-be turned to Roger. "I'll keep this house for you, Roger the First, and Tolly will do so after me. Where should we be if it was gone? And look, Roger, you keep this ring for me. It is a family heirloom. Keep it for your wife. It will come to me again."

"Mercy!" said Roger, dropping on one knee to receive it. "That's too hard to think, it makes my brain spin. But I will keep it, and it shall come back to you."

The leaves rustled and one by one began to slip off the tree, gliding down to the ground like vermilion feathers, as if the tree was preening itself. In a few days the diaphanous dome of their meeting place would be gone and only a winter skeleton tree be left in the sun. Roger heaved a great sigh, but he had been given a promise. He sat looking at the ring; then he drew in his breath, and without turning round he could smell the forest behind him and hear the gentle sighing of the breeze in the treetops. Before him spread the long view of the river valley with its narrow strips of plough and fallow, its commons and osier beds and orchards, and in the distance the new manor house, his own. He was one of many, but he was the first. They who received him so willingly were his descendants, even the grandmother! He laughed at that and set off home, taking deep lungfuls of the different scents, along banks where there were as many butterflies as flowers. It was good to be alive in a world that had room for all the thousand varieties of things that lived, where the sounds of men were the ring of an axe, the creak of a wagon, the slow rhythm of oars, the swish of a scythe, the squeak of the pump handle, or the church bell. All these sounds he could hear as he went toward home. No frightful monsters swooped out of the sky, no metal beetles whizzed along roads leaving a poisonous smell behind them. His village was as small in the endless countryside as the heronry in a far spinney. Coming home was bliss.

Roger showed his grandmother the glass bottle, which he told her truly he had found on the river bank. She was so amazed that he made her a present of it. She said that water was much more refreshing out of that than out of a leather bottle or a cowhorn. She wondered if even the queen had anything like it! It must have been dropped by some foreign merchant going up the river with treasures for the Bishop of Peterborough. He was said to live very luxuriously. The bottle had Roman lettering on it that she and Roger could not understand. NO DEPOSIT, NO RETURN and SCHWEPPES.

"But you have a ring on your finger that I have never seen before. Let me look."

The ring was gold set with a dark orange stone on which was incised the tiny figure of a Roman soldier with a spear and shield.

"Did you find that on the river bank, too?"

"No, I got it there," said Roger, pointing out of the window to where in the future the beech tree would be. "On that bank where the soil was heaped up out of the moat when it was dug out."

"You are lucky. Many things are dropped into water by accident but few are found again. Keep it, my dear. Don't give that away. It's your luck."

"I will, grandmother; you can be sure."

Eleven

For several days Roger was very happy at home, riding Viking, swimming with the pages or watching the craftsmen at work. For instance, the sculptor, who had carved out the Christ child and Saint Christopher's body and all the folds of his clothes, and was now with miraculous cunning carving out of stone transparent water with fishes swimming in it round Saint Christopher's legs. Or he watched Olaf, whose bright blue eyes looked at him piercingly and certainly saw his ring, but who asked no questions. Then there were the carpenter and the thatcher, and Roger took lessons from the fletcher, setting grey goose feathers in arrows of ash wood, which he trimmed with his knife.

His jousting lessons were going well. He had speared the quintain ring eight times out of ten and had been promoted to a larger wooden shield. His father had given him permission to get the gilder to paint his arms on it, d'Aulneaux quartered with de

Grey. Riding with this shield made Roger smile from ear to ear.

The nine days' wonder of his ring had died down among the family, but its presence on his finger was to him a perpetual reminder and a tug of wonder. The terrors of the air and the road and the suffocating lack of all the living things there should be began to seem as unreal as a nightmare, while on the contrary that so-much-lived-in old house seemed more real than itself now. "*Now*," he thought, "it hasn't any meaning, or not much."

So, one clear autumn day when the air was alive with leaves of all colors coasting about on the breeze, and the trees were rapidly stripping, Roger set off on Viking with a sack which he meant to fill with nuts from the hazel bushes on Roger's Island, where every twig held out polished twin nuts in decorated double cups, each nut a marvelous subtle shape between his fingers. He could crack the shells between his back teeth, and Watchet was eager and expert at it. Roger tethered Viking and picked a quarter of a sackful.

The Stones were gleaming in the clear blue autumn light. Their granular surface, if looked at closely, was many-colored, like precious stones in a mine not yet cut and polished. They stood out on the hill and there was nothing between them and the infinite blue except a few white clouds, innocent travelers fading as they went.

Roger, impressed with the dignity of the scene, bowed to the King Stone, and sat down, with no notion clearer than the great range of time before and behind him. After a while his thoughts concentrated to a wish.

"Tolly, my double. I want to see him again."

At once he was aware of a noise he had heard before in a nightmare. An inconceivable thing was coming along the track making the earth tremble. It had a sort of tower on top and it lurched and swam along the ground belching out black clouds. Roger leapt toward Viking who was sweating and rearing to get free, and he led him dancing sideways farther away down the other side of the hill where even Watchet had fled with his tail between his legs, but growling and red-eyed. From there Roger saw Tolly on a pony riding toward the monster, which had left the track, lurched and bucked across the shallow stream and was crawling up to the Stones. Tolly's pony was not concerned at all, and stood quietly while his rider shouted to the men sitting on the monster's neck. They quietened it and the noise and black smoke stopped. In the silence Roger shouted and beckoned, and Tolly waved back. He talked to the men and then

rode down to join Roger. Viking calmed down when an untroubled horse was beside him, though he still quivered.

"What ever is it?"

"It's a tractor with a crane. They've come to take the Stones away."

"Take the Stones away? *They can't.*"

"They can. They say they are to take them to the museum, because they are very old."

"Old!" said Roger with a groan. "Old! I should say they are."

He stood horrified while men jumped out of the thing and shouted orders. The noise started up again, and from the tower a long arm swung out with huge pincers at the end. These, after swaying about over it, came down and grabbed the Queen Stone, and with a roar and a jerk tore it out of the ground like pulling a tooth, swung it round, and lowered it into a truck at the back. It was done while Roger was still petrified with horror and disbelief. Then the arm came forward again and the King Stone, with two jerks and a fearful skidding sound of disaster and much shouting from the men, was up and swinging in the air. Roger found he could not even scream. He fainted.

When he came round, Tolly was splashing cold water on his face and Watchet licking his hand. All was silent. He made an effort to sit up. The dreadful thing was gone.

The quiet hill was streaked with shadows from the setting sun, but no shadows marked the presence of the Stones. Where they had been were two small gaping holes that would soon be grown over. Roger looked with tears running down his face.

"They were so old," he said, "and in their own places. Where have they been taken?"

"To the local museum, where old things are kept."

"But they were in their own place," Roger repeated. "Out of it they will be dead. It's a dreadful thing to do. As bad as sacking a church. And those men behaved like ruffians, the sort that drag people away to be killed." He got up and went to fondle Viking's nose and pull out pieces of grass that had got twisted round the bit. He turned melancholy eyes on Tolly.

"Do you take that sort of thing for granted?" he asked.

"It happens," Tolly answered. "But my grandmother and I do all we can to prevent it. She fights for Green Knowe every day of her life. We didn't know about this." Then he added sadly, "Now I shall never be able to come to you again. I shall never see your house as it was."

"As it *is*," said Roger, finding his wits again. "And that means I can see you again because *in my time* the Stones are still there."

He was alone, and the Stones were standing in their place, throwing long shadows before them.

Lucy Maria Boston (1892–1990) purchased a ramshackle manor house near Cambridge, England, in 1935, which over a period of two years she lovingly restored. It is this house that inspired her, at the age of sixty-two, to take pen in hand and create the beloved Green Knowe chronicles. L. M. Boston said she wrote her books to please herself—but the pleasure of her stories extends to all who read them.

VISIT GREEN KNOWE!

Lucy Boston wrote the Green Knowe stories about her own house and garden, located in Cambridgeshire, England. It is a very old house, built nearly nine hundred years ago, so it was easy for her to imagine the various children who may have lived there in the past. Lucy enjoyed showing the garden and the house to visitors, particularly those who had read the Green Knowe books, because they would recognize some of the things they had read about in the stories.

Although Lucy Boston died some years ago, her daughter-in-law, Diana Boston, welcomes guests to the house and offers guided tours by appointment. For more information, including directions, hours, and details on how to arrange a visit, please go to www.greenknowe.co.uk.